Praise for Lonesome

Lonesome Ballroom swept me right off my feet—
its giddy language and irresistible narrator leading me
in a wild dance of multigenerational myth-making.
Madeline McDonnell is a fearless and soulful original.

Sarah Shun-lien Bynum, author of *Likes*

Madeline McDonnell is a brilliant sound-worker,
and *Lonesome Ballroom* is a gleaming, teeming symphony of
a novel. What a magnificent dive into film, fashion, feminism,
motherdom, and the manifold performances that make up a life.

Leni Zumas, author of *Red Clocks*

Lonesome Ballroom totally dazzled and deranged me. Its prose is
a delight, by turns acrobatic, funny, and poetic, and its narrator,
Betty, is full of rage, longing, and a drive to tell her story—
even as she is undone by the narratives imposed on her.
I've long admired Madeline McDonnell's daring and beautiful
work, and I can't wait for the world to read this ingenious,
important novel. There is nothing like it—and it's a wonder.

Edan Lepucki, author of *Time's Mouth*

Madeline McDonnell's novel, *Lonesome Ballroom*,
is a beguiling conspiracy of beauty. Forgive me, did I say novel,
I mean bejeweled hand grenade. For *Lonesome Ballroom* is a
literary firestorm and every wondrous word a weapon against
the brooding brutes whose prideful and vainglorious tales

McDonnell muffles and mutes with a silk-gloved fist. In McDonnell's tour de force, her war-torn cri de coeur, we fall forever for Betty—a woman under the influence, a woman on the verge. But unlike Cassavetes or Almodóvar, McDonnell neither fears nor fetishizes femininity. She luxuriates in the daring glamour of her heroine's contradictions. Like the silent women in Cindy Sherman's film stills, Betty is a study in passive rage and rageful passivity. Betty is a fur coat of feral ermine, a ball gown of broken glass. Unabashed and unafraid, Betty emerges from the insidious glow of the dimming gaslight into her own fiery truth. Madeline McDonnell is a literary powerhouse.

Amber Dermont, author of *Damage Control*

Madeline McDonnell's *Lonesome Ballroom* is a novel that is also a ~~novel~~ about a girl who is also a ~~girl~~ in a world that is also a ~~world~~. Reading McDonnell is to watch a haunted, brilliant seamstress pull at the thread of the story she is telling and use what she's unraveled to tell the story she is untelling. What a gorgeous, weird book that completely redefines the borders of self-actualization, composition, and delight.

Sabrina Orah Mark, author of *Happily*

Madeline McDonnell's *Lonesome Ballroom* has gifted us Betty, a woman painfully in thrall to what every woman knows: that we are too often defined by what we are to others. Well, Betty refuses. The only way out is to smash everything to bits. Will she? Can she? I feel delightfully pulverized by this bright, desperate, mordantly funny voice.

Lindsay Hunter, author of *Hot Springs Drive*

LONESOME
BALLROOM

RESCUE PRESS

CHICAGO | CLEVELAND | IOWA CITY

LONESOME BALLROOM
Copyright © 2025 Madeline McDonnell
All rights reserved
Printed in the United States of America
FIRST EDITION
ISBN 979-8-9886839-0-2

Design by Sevy Perez
Graveur Variable
rescuepress.co

LONESOME BALLROOM

Madeline McDonnell

for the Leonas

Theme from Lonesome Ballroom

—Madeline McDonnell

(med. ballad)

Intro.
TUESDAY / 13

A
HOW I GOT HERE / 40

A
HOW I GOT HERE / 75

B
CRASH! / 145

A
HOW I GOT HERE / 197

Frank Ward
Ingrid Bergman in a 1961 Ford Comet, 2010
Archival pigment print, 33 x 22.9 cm / 13 x 9 in

Intro.
TUESDAY

1.

I wish I could start with the crash. The whirling windshield, the house twirling up as if from childhood, hurling itself toward the glass. Then—headlights pushing the bushes apart, flowers like cosmic flares. But I'm sorry. This story starts on a Tuesday.

I did the things one does in X on a Tuesday—the coffee, the toast, the brushing of coffee and toast from teeth. I drove to "work" without incident. I perched on a white chair behind a white desk. Latched the glass, went to lunch with E. And went home, ascending the hill without trouble.

Dinnertime! Duck à l'orange, Henry's favorite.

We sat.

We cut.

We chewed.

Well, Henry did—chewed, nodded, chewed; paused, considering. Only to nod with new vehemence—he was *really* eating now! He swallowed as if in confirmation, ah-ed as if relieved his proposition had proved sound. Then? He arranged his features to feature the pleasure his nods and ahs presupposed. Or so I assume. By the time Henry said "Are you serious?" my eyes were on the table.

It was teak, with a straight, subtle grain, the meanest, cleanest lines, not a Jens Risom original, but nonetheless an—

"*Id*iot! I've been thinking we should bring a baby into this. I'm an idiot! But you promised. You said it was the paaaaaaghst—"

The table was no Risom original, fair enough, but Henry didn't have to pound his fists on it. And the mortal vowel sounds were a bit much. "I'm sorry. I'm really not thinking about—"

I was thinking about the table, I swear, looking at it, and at my plate, admiring the varnish on both teak and duck. The duck à l'orange, which was every bit as delicious as Henry's performance implied, though my portion was a little salty, and a little damp, and, fine, fine, there were skin crisps floating, little puddles...

"Then why are you crying, Betty? Why are you crying again?"

2.

X is one of those New England pseudocities unrepentant about preservation; its residences feature bootscrapers and brass doorknockers, low-ceilinged room-boxes that still seem to flicker with gaslight. I was sitting in just such a room that Tuesday, and I had no ostensible reason to rage. I was youngish, for whatever that's worth, blondish, for whatever, etc., awash in material comfort. I had that table! Plus two parents, who happened to live next door. A house, a Henry—first comes love, then comes marriage—

So what if I was living through a non-era that would be deemed a dark age a few years hence? So what if mine was a generation that would never merit a name, the one whose antiwar parents had started a war that would never end? So what if explosives I could see but never hear traced their way across the same screen traipsed across by spring-breaking coeds seconds later, words like "liberated" and "peaches" stitched across each velour ass? And so what if—amid all these post-, but not yet post-post-, systems and theories and systems theories—the ostensible thing to me was the table?

I was only twenty-ugh. I worked the same job I'd scored at twenty-two and the one thing that had changed at the gallery in ~~several some~~ not so many years was my boss. By the Tuesday in question, it was E. Yes, *E*. My old gossipmate. My old getting-it-mate. My roommate at the distinguished institution I shall hereupon refer to as "the U." But so what? I was used to seeing my onetime classmates in the gallery.

Jenny Oeuf, for example, who had thrown up every morning before Orgo and yet now popped up most mornings in my inbox, because if I believed it was time for a new generation of Democratic leadership shouldn't I chip in a buck or twenty to her campaign? And Calliope Pandey, whose strenuously restrained reports on our nation's unrestrained military ops did their best to desecrate my pristine screen. And not least Sarah Smalls, whose chipmunky grin, interrogative gaze, and child-size waist had won her a series of increasingly terrific roles in a series of increasingly horrific summer blockbusters. In fact, I'd been watching paparazzi footage of Sarah that Tuesday. Watching as she lifted a bagel to laughing lips, then thought better of it, reached out as if to offer it to me. Or to E? My best-friend-turned-boss was standing with her hands on my chairback, after all. Saying, "Let's go to lunch! This is *too* weird."

Fair enough. But here's the thing. Whatever pathetic, partial-life crisis I may or may not have been having at work that morning, or at lunch with E come afternoon, was incidental to the puddle on my plate that night, to the tremble of teak as I crashed, smashed, or, at very least, pushed, my chair in. ("Are you seriously storming out?" Henry cried, delighted.) It was incidental to the puny kapow of the driver's-side door, incidental to the foot that felt for the brake, the fist that found its way to Reverse. It didn't cause the houses to blink yellow goodbyes, the treetops to fly past like some dark flock. Didn't turn College Street to Scholar Street to Gown, which would take me all the way down. It didn't turn on the neon woman who sung out L-O-N-E-S-O-M-E B-A-L-L-R-O-O-M, didn't open the bar's portholed door.

3.

Cut to ~~several some~~ not so many months before. To the first time I noticed the woman who switched on in the sky, dress stitched out of cold cathodes. I'd driven that stretch countless times. How had I never seen the blue letters she sang, the eighth notes that tumbled from her lips toward the door?
  Anyway, I followed them.
  Inside, the bar was black-and-white. The music was low and strange, an orchestra tuning up. Dust motes drifted, and the soundtrack shifted, an overture shimmering out of the static as a tall dark figure zoomed into view behind the bar.
  Peekaboo hair. A frown fixed in place by femme fatale lipstick. I might have taken her for a vision out of Hollywood's Golden Age had it not been for the t-shirt with its savagely scissored collar, some band name stretched illegible across the breast. Her dangly earrings had demanded the decapitation of two Barbie dolls. She looked at me, I opened my mouth—
  "I got her, Lizzie." A new tall, dark someone was beside me, smiling as if he'd been waiting. "She'll have the usual," this one said. I'd never seen him before.
  But the barmaid was already shaking out an icy rhythm on a silver cylinder, shaking her head at me because the man— Goodman—was taking off the little screens of his glasses, looking

me up and down, putting them back on and taking my hand, leading me in a tumbling two-step to his table. I was sitting on theater velour then, and he was introducing me to Jim, a ghosty Classics all-but-PhD defined by little but his lack of definition, he might have been twenty or forty, everyone called him Sunshine. And then Goodman was doing as a good Goodman should, taking his own seat, talking at me like he knew me. He was telling the one about his grandfather's golden retriever—how Fluffernutter had saved little Goodman from drowning, swinging into the swimming hole on a vine she managed to clench between her teeth!—and the next thing I knew it was bar time. Then it was seven or three, it was five o'clock somewhere, it was the next night and the next. The past was crashing into the present because it was the next month already—it was September then November then March—it was Sunday, Monday—and Goodman was on a roll, talking Fluffernutter's grandpup, Fluffer*mutt*er, talking *Moby Dick* or Maddux's mastery of the outside corner—

The magnificence of the Muscle Shoals Rhythm Section, and, to think, they were all white guys!—

The Marantz Model 2 tube amps built into his great-uncle's great room, fucking sweet!—

Which meant the months had flipped to June, and it was Tuesday. That Tuesday just under two decades ago, the day on which I dared depart from house and husband before dinner or dishes were done, before said husband was even decommissioned by DVD, the day on which I am so sorry to start my story. Ah!: to slam out, to speed down, to leave Henry in the paaaaaghst and lose myself in the Lonesome, where conversation didn't require speech and friendliness didn't require friendship, where I was an unknown, a no one, a nothing nothing nothing nothing nothing, where my blasted, glass-faced tablemates didn't even seem to know my—

"Betty?" Goodman leaned across the table. "Are you crying?"

4.

And so what if I'd stormed, slammed, sped in order to escape this exact line of inquiry? When Goodman pursued it that Tuesday—"You *sure* you're okay? Whatever's going on, you can tell us!"—I knew what to say, or what not to:

Goodman and Sunshine did not want the whole truth, and they did not want my meet-cute. They did not want to hear that I'd married the literal boy-next-door, that I'd seen him for the first time ~~several~~ some not so many Septembers ago, that I'd been standing on my parents' front porch, trying to light a cigarette. They didn't want to know that Henry was standing on his, a hand shading his eyes, so that he might better stare contemplatively into the distance, and they certainly didn't care that he'd worn frayed khakis and a collared shirt, a tweed jacket with actual leather patches at the elbows, that his abstracted gaze was as intentionally professorial as his dress, that he sighed as if to indicate the great weight of his intellect, that I laughed, that our eyes met, that I took in the fated face for the first time, its perfection marred poignantly by the strain of needing to be watched, that the tall dark handsome stranger who was my neighbor summoned a desperate smile, that I rolled my eyes even as sympathy filled me, even as I felt myself falling in—

"You can trust us, Betty!" Goodman gave his glass a musical shake. "What's your story?"

But Goodman and Sunshine did not want to hear that after ~~several~~ some not so many years, the very qualities that had drawn me to my husband—his easy-uneasy good looks, the sweet eagerness of his performance of himself—Henry Block stars in *Henry Block: A Biopic*!—now repelled me. They didn't want a scene set at a teak table, Jens Risom original or no—first comes love, then comes marriage, then comes the duck à l'orange in the—

But Goodman and Sunshine didn't want to hear, as Henry claimed to, about cycles of the extrahistorical or extra-major-league variety, about the consistency of my vaginal discharge and its implications re: ovulation calculations, about the baby who might appear as a result of said sums, the baby I couldn't help but imagine as a miniature husband, performing his goos and coos with a desolating and unnatural will—o khaki, collared mini-man, with his wacky, elbow-patched onesie! No, I'd been listening, and Goodman and Sunshine didn't go in for unnecessary details of dress. Moreover, fond as they were of bad fathers, I wasn't supposed to slander my would-be baby's!

Fortunately for Goodman and Sunshine, *Henry* was the last word in the world I wished to say that Tuesday, the very last name I intended to take in vain.

I would take this one, instead: *Orson.*

5.

The problem? I could only get to Orson by way of the biopic.

Starring, yep, the man I've claimed I will not name as…

The Man I've Claimed I Will Not Name!

Ambitious Academic!

Diligent Duckeater!

Why not add *Devoted Dogowner* to my husband's casting breakdown?

Sure, sure, there had been certain, ahem, stresses of late, but so what? A dog would move us past that paaaaaaghst, into our familial future. And so what if our star had never fed one walked one bathed one brushed one picked up the shit of, etc.? ~~Henry~~, I mean, H—can I call my husband Boyfriend H for just a moment?—just knew he'd love a dog!

Picture, then, the classic scene: Dog (Male/Neutered, Labrador

Retriever, Three Years, Three Months) and Devoted Dogowner (Male I've Claimed I Will Not Hail, Professor, Thirty-Three Years) taking to the lawn on their first sky-blue afternoon together, two months prior to the Tuesday in question. Grandly, Devoted Dogowner lengthens an arm, releases a gleaming Frisbee into the breeze. Communion is nigh! For his new best friend is fixing on the disc, ears hanging close to his head, lush as the flaps of the hat in which, ~~not so~~ many years before, my grandmother had me watch *Dr. Zhivago*. Zoom in. Dog's eyes are hazel, and in possession of a frictive flicker not unlike said grandmother's. But why do they look so...wet? Those aren't—no, they can't possibly be—tears forming at the corners—can they? And why does Dog just sit-stay-stare up at the sky as his would-be BFF's glimmering offering flies by? Labs are famed for their friendly energy, so why does this one make a sound that is less bark than cry—*errrrrrrrr, errrrrrrrr*—why does he drop down, dejected, then curl up like a cat in the grass? Why does he make the man fetch the Frisbee himself?

Errrrrrrr! the dog answers.

Devoted Dogowner fetches, scratches his head with the Frisbee's edge. Then smiles like he's had a revelation. Nods. *Errrrrrrr!* He agrees!

That's when both Dog and Devoted, Man and Best Friend, look up at the porch, where I stand as if awaiting their cue. And that's when I hear it: not *errrrrrrrr* but *herrrrrrrrr*!

Am I just imagining that Dog points his tail at me?

In any case, I say "Sure!" when H explains that he's had an idea, and will I fill in with Orson for just a minute while he jots it down?

"Orson?"

Oh yeah! H passes me the Frisbee as we pass on the porch steps. Don't I think we should call our little buddy Orson?

I repeat my line, suresuresure, why *not* name this quietly *herrrrrrrr*ing, depressive cat of a dog, who is everything a Labrador's not supposed to be, for a raucous, imperious, utterly undeterrrrrrrrred man? Director and star not just of *Citizen Kane* but also the "free-form documentary," *F for Fake*, about which H happens to be ideating for the next just-a-minute, turned twenty, thirty, forty? So what? I fling, Orson the Dog fetches. When the sun sets, I lead him to water—to sweet patch of sun, setting on the floor as I cook—to teak table, beneath which I drop scrap after unchewed scrap—to couch, where, at last, we sit beside H, watching Orson's namesake drink. Orson the Man drinks and smokes and eats, and drinks and eats and smokes some more, and wears silly white gloves and a silly black hat, all while expounding upon narcissism and charlatanism with a maniacal glee I'd expect to unsettle my own man. But H leans forward, rapt. I lean back, wondering when it might be possible to slip out to the Lonesome and make like Orson Senior, wondering whether it will ever be possible to leave Junior, who is *herrrrrrrrr*ing beside me still, in the care of careless H.

"Ours, the scientists tell us, is a universe that's disposable," Orson the Man intones from the screen.

I take Welles's cue this time, push my way to the rim of the couch. But no sooner have I shifted my weight away from Junior's than he is up and on me, paws on thighs, eyes unrelentingly knowing on my own. *Heeeeeeeerrr*, he whines, *here, I'm here*, and his tongue is too, on my nose and mouth; my face is wet, cheeks, chin, neck, he's going for the eyes now. I close them, as sympathy fills me, as I feel myself falling, aaahh!

But open those eyes and the *aaahh* is just H, heaving his performative approval—H, looking at me like I'm in some sort of Pietà rather than beneath the weight and wet tongue of his property, this dog he just knew he'd—

"I just knew you'd love a dog!" he says. Grave reversal, but so what? It's only when he ups the ante, tries, "It'll be good for you to have a baby," that we get the dump-thump, the kkkksssshhh, the kapow. "What?" I say, and he repeats, "good for you to have a hobby," but it's too late, I've already pushed without bidding myself to push, and Junior hits the floor with a sick crack, limbs splaying strangely. *Herrrrrrrrr!?*

No, not *herrrrrrrrr*: *himmmmmmmmmm*! Junior is the problem, Junior! Not you, but the baby in my brain with Block's biopic face—its desolating diligence, its contented intent—

I put my hand to my own, and it is wet, so wet—it's almost as if Orson is on me again, my cheeks and chin are dripping, but no, the dog's only licking his own paws, and H is looking up from the floor where he is attempting, tentatively, to tend, saying, "Are you seriously doing this again? I don't—"

6.

"—get it. Do you, Sunshine?"

"Not really. I mean, that was supposed to be a dog story, right? But what was the thing about *Dr. Zhivago*? I lost you there, Betty. Your grandma had some kind of hat?"

"Not that." Goodman leaned my way until I was inside the minimovie his glasses made. "You'd be a *great* mom! So what if you don't want a dog? Don't you want a baby?"

And so what if I'd come to the Lonesome to escape this exact line of interrogation? I was also a good student, and by the Tuesday in question I'd been listening to Goodman for months, and I was pretty sure I could give him the answer he wanted—yes, I was almost positive I could get it right if I just—

"Oh shit, Betty, what did I say? You *are* crying! Why are you crying?"

7.

Picture it! Picture the paaaaaaghst—picture X in 1976.

Picture a stately saltbox colonial—erected in 1776, painted avocado green two hundred years hence—where the Mrs.—oh the poor Mrs.!—still lives. Picture a picnic table, a pile of ransacked presents, smashed-in boxes and smushed cake.

Have we arrived at the Bettian ur-scene? Have we gone back along the matriarchal line in order to find that scene or gene that might merit a song, or explain my distress, or start some sort of story?

The thing is: Goodman was sorry for prying. Or maybe he was sorry for violating our tacit rhetorical tenets, for requesting the speech he'd implicitly pledged to give? Either way, I didn't need to answer.

"Listen, Betty! I get it. I'll never be a father, and it's one of *the* great sadnesses of my life. No, but listen, listen! Mine's a dog story too."

So picture it. Picnic table, present pile. Sun-yellow Super-8 colors. Goodman turns nine today. You can just make him out at the far end of the lawn, standing, lifting something long.

It's a rifle. And this is a story central to the Goodmanian canon, so soon that rifle will go off.

The suspense builds as the perspective moves closer, Goodman the younger growing taller... Picture his grass-stained sneakers, his mussed hair, his tiny hands trembling on the gun. He's always wanted a rifle, so why are tears blurring his face even as it comes into focus? And what is that doomed form beside the fence? A buck? A doe? No, a dog.

Goodman raises the rifle, tears and snot streaming. A man's voice screaming, "Do it, boy!"

Steady, steady... He aims, because he's asked for this, hasn't he? His fingers are numb and his hands are too small, his skin sticky, but somehow he—

I had come to the Lonesome Ballroom for this—this singular ideal discourse, this friendliness that didn't require friendship, this conversation that was perfect precisely because it did not require me to speak. So why were Goodman and Sunshine swiveling, looking at me as if I had?

"Exactly," Goodman said. "My ninth birthday."

Picture it. The dark forest that fringes the property, the blue triangles the trees draw upon the sky, the undergrowth that seems fashioned of shadow. Goodman follows his father, trains his eyes on the floating ghost of his old man's t-shirt, tries to keep from his mind the other specters that lurk here, the specter they are bringing in now, the dog's body bloody in his father's arms, the tail hanging limp, or askew somehow, what's different about it—? No! Don't look, little Goodman... That climax has passed. Time to put the event away—slam the door, shut the drawer, etc.—the way all good Goodmen do.

But then Goodman trips and sees it: the tiny cross, two twined twigs. Then he sees another—and another—

"But don't you get it?" Sunshine was talking as if I'd asked for clarification. "They're graves, Betty."

Goodman shook his head. "I can't even tell you how many... Dad had killed Fluff's parents, and Gramps had killed her grandparents—"

"Not Fluffernutter?" Sunshine said.

"Fucking Fluffernutter." Goodman shook his head.

"Please tell me *some* died of natural causes."

"You know I'd love to, Sun. But I'm afraid—"

And I loved this, didn't I, this friendliness that didn't require friendship, this conversation that didn't—

Again, Goodman and Sunshine swiveled their somber heads. They were right to, because I loved this, I swear, I totally, totally loved it, and, yes, I needed just this sort of distracting, ridiculous

story on the Tuesday in question, so why was I crying, "Come *on*!"?
More importantly, had Lizzie Barmaid heard?

8.

She was close enough, certainly. She was eyeing our empties, mouth ajar, tray balanced on one arm. I didn't remember ever actually introducing myself to Lizzie, didn't remember telling the barmaid about my tenuous tenure in what passed in X for an art world, though I must have, at some point, because there she always was, hovering stern and sudden above, everything she wasn't asking me aloud blaring through her glare.

Could she get me another? And could I give her a break? Were these assholes actually making me cry? And what was I—Betty B. of the pseudo-venerable Snodgrass Gallery—doing *here* in the first place?

The truth was—

But no, I couldn't say it to Lizzie's face.

I could say this, though: "Come on, dude, seriously!"

I could say something Lizzie would appreciate: "That story is, like, right out of a Guy Greco movie."

The heads swiveled once more.

"'Cupper, you indigent fuck!'" Goodman said.

"'You can take your ball, Dad. I don't want your fucking ball,'" Sunshine answered.

Goodman now: "'The briefcase was fireproof.'"

Sunshine, gruffly: "'That's good.'"

"'My ass wasn't.'"

"'That's bad.'"

They laughed. Looked at me, looked at each other, laughed louder.

"I take it you're not a *Brutal/Sensitive* fan, Betty?"

"Is it even out?"

"You've seen his other stuff, though? I mean, you have to have seen *Sweatpoison*?"

"*Fatherfucker*?"

I knew the titles. Indeed, I knew Guy Greco's IMDB page as well as I knew which dress Sarah Smalls had worn to her most recent premiere, a frothy whip of tulle dyed the color of mint chocolate chip, its bodice embellished with paillettes, pearls, sequins, and seed beads, its semi-sweetheart neckline finished in—

Anyway, I knew it well.

I may even know it still.

9.

According to the Internet Movie Database, Guy Greco has no fewer than seven films in development. In his headshot, he wears his usual flannel, and—even within the wee-est telephonic screen—his sideburns seem inches long. His eyes manage to bug out as they narrow, so strenuous is his appraisal. It's a relief to scroll through to the other images, to let Guy Greco turn his restive and captious gaze away. He is busy, after all. He is standing on the set of *Men in Pain*, extending a long stiff lens. Or he is obscuring his flannel with a scarf of camel cashmere, he is staring, disgusted, at the glassine hunk in his hand—the audience award he's just picked up in Zurich or Utah or Dubai for *Matt Eats a Sandwich*. In the next frame, he is tuxedoed but still untamed, those sideburns sculpted into magnificent wildness, one arm struggling to drape itself about the massive shoulders of Jake Rock, the actor who has been with our own GG since well before *The Woodsman*, the short that started it all.

The Woodsman was shot not so many years before the Tuesday in question. Guy Greco had made the film for a first-semester MFA seminar, then submitted it to festivals on what he called an "anti-lark." He knew it would win, and it did: it won Best Independent Mini-Feature at a festival or fifty; it won special praise ("Ballsy!") for the seventeen straight minutes Jake Rock spends standing before a cracked mirror, shaving moss ("That's right: *moss*!") from his face; it won the notice of Popper Ashburnham, the powerful art-horror producer; and it won the artist formerly known as Greck his first job helming a feature.

Of course, by the Tuesday in question, Greck had disavowed that feature—*Get Along Home, Betsy, Betsy*—as "dickless schlock." What was not to renounce? Guy Greco had not conceived its conceit (When a group of high-school football players invite the titular—not to mention virginal!—new girl to a weekend rager at a grizzly preserve, terror ensues... But who is responsible for the dead revelers: the bears, the boys, or Betsy!?). He had not scripted its script ("What big arms you have," Betsy, Betsy coos to the presumed wide receiver in an early scene, "and they're furry!"). But he had been "ballsier!" enough to close said schlock with an eight-minute single-take tracking shot—no edits! no cuts!—following a mystery character out of the depths of a windy cave; into the infrared woods; through a shootout between the alcoholic sheriff and a renegade tight end (Jake Rock, in a rare minor role); in and out of the burned-out shell of the team's travel bus; over two barbed-wire fences; and, finally, to the lighted window of Betsy, Betsy's cabin. Inside, Betsy, Betsy—played by who else but our own Sarah Smalls?—sits on a ratty couch, her large eyes closed, her neck erect, her hand moving languorously beneath her skirt. The camera thrusts in, out, in, as, through the crescendo of Betsy, Betsy's moans, we discern another sound, a soft thlunk-thlunk-thlunking. The glass clouds. The cloud dissolves. Betsy, Betsy dissolves, ecstatic. Thlunk. Thlunk. The camera pans swiftly back, and we see an enormous grizzly bear—we've occupied his perspective all along!—thrusting his wet nose against the pane.

It was Guy Greco's willingness "not just to enter the mind and body of a predator, but to reveal the soft longing within" that led Ashburnham to finance the former's first big-budget foray as auteur, *Brutal/Sensitive*. On the Tuesday in question, *B/S* had been in theaters for two weeks. No, Goodman, no, Sunshine—please believe me, Lizzie!—I had not seen it. But I had seen Guy on my screen, shilling his soul—his words. "It's weird to be here," his beard said to a bendy, pompadoured late-night host. "I mean, this project is, like, *me*, you know? It's not a *product*."

As he spoke, he looked angrily at the camera. Which had me cutting to not so many years before, to a not so distant classroom at the U, to Guy Greco casting just that angry look at the series of shoeboxes I'd boldly titled *Death* and turned in for my Image and Communication critique, at the dolls' clothes I'd painstakingly disarranged within. His sneer was so pure—you'd have thought his disgust would be canceled out by the pleasure he took in it, but instead it was elevated, enhanced.

"Is this, like, a comment on capitalism?" Guy Greco asked, as he examined my scrupulously reconstructed dressing rooms, which were not comments but memories, memorials, maybe. My grandmother, who'd died not so many days before, had taken me to such spaces throughout my stupid childhood. "I *know*. And that's cool," Guy said, "but, like, I don't think it's working? I mean, maybe if you privilege *commenting* over narrative content. But what's the point? We've all read Judith Butler—gender performance, commodification, blah blah. But what's the point if no one wants to look? If no one wants to *keep* looking, I mean... I'm sorry, but it's a dressing room. Like, in a mall. Sure, I get it, we're all empty, commerce is empty, we're all complicit, but what's your *story*?"

10.

Cut back to Tuesday. By which I mean cut ahead. To the Lonesome Ballroom, where, fine, fine, I was at very least crying out. Raising my voice at Goodman, in hopes that the hovering Lizzie Barmaid would hear. "So I haven't seen *Brutal/Sensitive*!" I cried. "So what? I've seen enough of his 'flicks' to know that you just narrated the Guy Greco ur-scene. *You* know, the hero's face goes hazy and he's a kid again and his dad's yelling at him to go ahead and bludgeon their pet parrot, or whatever. I swear there's always some climactic dead animal..."

Goodman's voice was mild. "I can't think of any."

"Well, there *is* the Komodo dragon in *Bloodletting*," Sunshine said. "That's kind of an esoteric example, though."

"Shit. I stand corrected. Plus, I guess the pets do die at the beginning of *Brutal/Sensitive*. The dalmatian, the gecko... But that scene *isn't* the climax."

"Yeah, but she does *kind* of have a point if you're counting *Betsy, Betsy...*"

"You gotta count *Betsy*!"

"And, I don't know, the rabbit in *Sweatpoison*?"

"*Oh* yeah... And isn't there a dog in *Fatherfucker*?"

"Two. Corgis, I think? Actually, doesn't Rye Wrecko smother them on his eighteenth birthday?"

"Dude! That scene's incredible!"

"But, like you said, it's not the climax. I don't know, though, do you think it presages the final sequence? With the ice cream truck? And the twelve-point buck?"

"Either way, it's absurd!" The heads swiveled again. "I mean, what is that trope even about?"

Sunshine, whose all-but-dissertation considered "epic paratext" in Homer and Hesiod, was delighted I'd deferred to his expertise.

29

"Oh," he said, mouth rounded in faux-surprise, "it can be traced to the *Odyssey*, at least! The death of Argos? *This is the dog who died when his master traveled out into the world...*"

Actually, Sunshine, the Goodmanian rhetorical and Grecan cinematic weren't the only canons with which I was familiar, so—had I come to the Lonesome Ballroom to speak—I might have reeled off the words that were reeling up from Classics 930, which I'd taken ~~several some~~ not so many years ago: *If you could only see the dog as he was when Odysseus abandoned him... so strong and swift you'd be amazed...*

Sunshine raised his translucent eyebrows at Goodman, who barked a laugh. As a voice—a wild, riled voice—a voice that was sliding toward stridence—said, "But he himself nears death now that his master has perished...and the women are too careless to take care of him!"

Fine, fine: it was my voice. So shut up, Betty! You came here to listen, and you know what not to say, so why are you shouting out the answer before Sunshine can, blurting those old words up at Lizzie as if your fluency in the paaaaaaghst might do anything but condemn you? "Servants are always like that—"

Cue Ms. Barmaid! Who was taking matters, or at least empties, into her own hands, thlunk-thlunk-thlunking them onto her tray, eloquent eyes persisting:

Seriously, Betty, what are you doing here?

Don't you have any other story to tell, or listen to, or live out?

"All right," Goodman said, "okay, impressive, Bets, especially after, let's see, four, five, six drinks! But you won't show this guy up. Sunshine's told you what his dad used to make him do, right?"

But Sunshine didn't have to, because, ah, at last, Goodman was doing as a good Goodman should, he was telling me himself, and I loved this, I swear I loved this, loved hearing about sadistic Sunshine, Sr., the quizzes he'd give on Sunshine's birthday—the first eleven lines from each of the major Western epics when he turned eleven, the first sixteen when he turned, etc.! Just as I loved the swift shift back from the arms and the man, from dogs and birds feasting on the bodies of heroes, to Goodman's birthday party. He's turning six this time and Goodman, Sr., has thrown the younger's presents down the stairs and now he's punching in the hall wall because, what, Lizzie? Don't you love it? How can you not love it!? Come on, Lizzie! We don't even have to listen, because we already know what he's saying, know what story he sings, know that this latest Goodman's wrath can be traced all the way to Goodman the First. And what could be more restful? We don't have to listen to know that we've plunged back into the paaaaaaghst, that Goodman the First or Third or Fifty-third is searching a shantytown for a deranged war buddy or dilettante ward. That Goodman the Second, or Fourth, or Forty-second is kicking heroin with the help of a purehearted waitress.

Or committing suicide on the anniversary of his father's death! Or hitting for the cycle whilst contemplating social cycle theory! Or wrapping a wounded blackbird in a bandana and gazing upon it with a tenderness he's never shown his son!

We know that Goodman the Seventh is weeping over the fate of Goodman the Eighth—oh poor doomed Goodman the Eighth, that dead little brother! *We* know him—the talented one, the handsome one, the one who is, alas, drinking grain alcohol at seven a.m., and setting fire to the tenement, and coming this close to killing their poor mother, oh poor Mrs. Goodman, who has every excuse to get back in bed and never get up, except she'll never do that because there are mouths to feed and sheets to wash and, well, she is just too tough.

And we know that Goodman the Ninth is scraping a flattened ear from the bottom of his field boot, or letting slip the secret of his second family, or ordering a lobotomy for his feeble-minded daughter, or flying his seventy-seventh sortie. We know that Goodman the Seventy-seventh has just made a staggering dagger shot, before fucking the lustful neighbor girl until she begs for more, before reading six different biographies of Castro, before climbing back over the sixteen-foot fence because he doesn't want to leave the asylum!

We know the words.

We've heard them all night, we've heard those same words all our lives.

So what's the harm, Lizzie? What's the terrible harm in hearing that Goodman the Sixth or Twelfth or Googooplexian has forced his seven-year-old son to gut a deer dog donkey toucan polliwog, has traversed all of Stockholm in just his stocking feet whilst decrying his own fraudulence, has watched his best friend's blasted hand fly—goodbye!—through the blue, has developed a necessary vaccine or unnecessary literary theory, or slit his wrists with a dull knife from the prep school refectory, or invented the cotton-gin group-shaving-machine artificial-brain-liver-heart, or decamped to an abandoned campsite in order to do *so* many drugs? I mean, sure, maybe we already know about his professional potential and his pay grade and his patents... Maybe we have always known and will ever know how horrifically hard it is to be some father's son, but is it really so hard for *us* to sit quietly inside the story once more?

Lizzie?

Lizzie?

II.

I don't remember when I found out she was a grad student in Media Studies at the institution that counted my alma mater as its archrival. I don't remember when I learned she was writing her dissertation on Cindy Sherman and Chantal Akerman. I don't remember when I discovered just how much we had in common, just how comfortable I should have felt in Lizzie Barmaid's presence.

It didn't matter. Anyway, by that time, I was comfortable.

An Old Fashioned appeared before me. Sunshine got it, or Goodman. I never had to ask, let alone make my own way to the bar. I never even had to say hello.

But Lizzie said it. "Hello, Charles. Hello, James." She was the only denizen of the Lonesome to call Goodman and Sunshine by their staid first names.

"Queen Elizabeth," Goodman would answer, "I am but your servant, so far be it from me to offer counsel, but this delightful beverage should be stirred, not shaken!"

"Above my pay grade, Charlie."

I could always feel Lizzie before I saw her. Before she'd so much as swiped her arm across the scarred wood she was required to wipe down, I'd feel my chin tilt, my lids drop. Through the fringe of my lashes, I'd see my gold face in my glass. I'd open my mouth, and hear the brisk kiss of her voice in place of my own. "Jimbo. Chuck." She never said anything to me.

"Don't mind Lizzie," Sunshine said one night. "She's not really friends with girls. You know the type, right?"

I made a scoff-like sound that meant I didn't. It seemed unseemly to admit I was conversant in his rhetoric.

"She doesn't mean anything by it. She might even like you!"

"It's okay," I said, and it was. By this time, I was comfortable with the discomfort Lizzie's visits occasioned. I knew the rule: at Goodman's table, there was room for only one of us.

12.

But then one day she talked. It was sunset, and I was stumbling toward the Lonesome's portholed door when I saw her. She was standing on the sidewalk, trying to light a cigarette, when the sign-woman's silent song switched on—L for Lizzie, then O, then N—turning the barmaid a beautiful blue.

"Hey," she said.

"Hey."

I hadn't taken the car to the bar, and my calves were throbbing. I held a pair of newish heels in one hand. Lizzie narrowed her eyes at them, and why not?

I knelt, placed the heels on the pavement, untied my sneakers as if she'd dared me. The heels had shimmered to life on the screen I stared and stared at in the gallery. One click and they were mine, Judy Garland singing "The Man That Got Away" from another open window, Sarah Smalls recommending Chanel Nailballet from a third. The shoes were red. They made me think of roses—the stem-bend of the arch, the whorl blossoming open at the toe. It felt good to slip them on, even hunched on the sidewalk, Lizzie and the Lonesome lady looming. I snuck my sneaks into my oversized purse. Or no, I didn't sneak. Lizzie Barmaid hadn't looked away. "Those look *so* uncomfortable. You looked cute in the sneakers. No one's gonna kick you out for wearing them..."

Kneeling had me level with Lizzie's snakeskin booties, which weren't exactly lacking in heel. She saw me looking.

Yeah, her eyes said. *The difference is I'm getting paid.*

"I worship your mother," her mouth added.

"Oh!" I said. "Um, thanks?"

13.

I didn't remember mentioning that my mother was Violet Flowers, yes *that* Violet Flowers—famed feminist frescoist, archfoe to Michelangelo—but I must have, at some point, because there I was not so many days later, watching the same mouth—Lizzie Barmaid's mouth—utter the famous moniker inside the Lonesome mirror.

I was wearing a red dress with strawberry-shaped buttons, trying to still my mouth with matching lipstick. Lizzie's lips were bare, but something delicate glinted from her left nostril. And when I let my eyes flit up, I faced the expert architecture of her arches, brows plucked to beguile.

"Violet Flowers! I mean, fuck. *The Creation of Violet* changed my life. I'm sure everyone says that to you. And I know the backlash. But I think it's more subversive *because* it's obvious. Not to mention honest! Don't pretend you can obliterate ten thousand years of patriarchy in, like, twenty, you know? At least your mom doesn't pander."

The Lonesome's two bathrooms resembled bombed-out craters. Inside, the walls careened even when you weren't drunk, graffiti detonating from some unspecified center. There were no mirrors in those bathrooms, no sinks. So when Lizzie searched the glass for some sign that I was *that* Violet Flowers's daughter—some dim but nimble glimmer of the unpandering candor within—we stood by the single sink in the back hallway. Anyone could have walked in on us.

"Did you go to the U?" she asked.

Yes indeed, I said, ~~several~~ some not so many years ago!

"Wait. So, like, you were there at the same time as Guy Greco? Don't tell Goodman that, he'll lose his shit. Anyway. I *just* read an interview with him, don't ask me why!"

"Well, *I* called him Greck..."

She looked at me.

"I mean, everyone did. Everyone called him Greck."

Then she looked away, leaned toward her own face. Took a tiny tube from her pocket and squirted. Dabbed a finger to her cheek, then to the bridge of her nose.

"Well, *I* think your friend *Greck* is full of shit. I mean, this interview was in *ArtAgora*, so I thought—ugh, I don't know what I thought. Same old shit. The big spread of him staring moodily at a sequoia... And then he goes on and on about the shotgun he got on his thirteenth birthday. I mean, come on, dude! Everyone knows you went to the U and had a trust fund and, like, a *Jules and Jim* poster over your bed."

Lizzie Barmaid didn't know the half of it, had no way of knowing that the poster on Greck's dorm wall had actually—

"And his rhetoric is *so* problematic. Like, he wants his films to 'bludgeon' his audience. That's why he has to write his screenplays so fast, to get that 'urgent brutality' in. So he writes them standing up at the workbench in his garage, except he doesn't say 'write,' it's 'punch out another screenplay' or 'bitch-slap a concept until it begs him to stop.' I mean, just imagine if, like, *I* did that! Or, oh my god, *you*, what if *you* were a filmmaker and you did that?"

"Did what?"

"*You* know! Performed your insanely normative hyperfemininity. It wouldn't work. Like, you couldn't wear *that* dress and talk about how you got a Peaches 'n Cream Barbie for your fifth birthday and how you write your screenplays at your dressing table or whatever."

"I guess it's a good thing I'm not a filmmaker!"

"'Where does the violence come from, Mr. Greco?' I mean, has anyone ever asked you where the *passivity* comes from?"

Lizzie picked at something on her forehead, ran her finger over a single magnificent brow. I waited, but her show had stopped as suddenly as it began. If anyone had walked in, they wouldn't have thought Lizzie Barmaid had talked to me at all.

14.

But cut to the Tuesday in question, and there was no question. Which is to say: there were only questions:

Are these assholes making you cry?
Did Violet Flowers raise you for this?
Don't you have anything better—anything other—?
The neon woman beamed her blue melody through the porthole. I closed my eyes but could still see her letters flicker in turn—on and off, off and on—a call someone kept failing to answer. I could still feel the dizzy rhythms of Lizzie's eyes, her silent line chiming in time.
Where the fuck does the passivity come from?
Had I really had four (and a-five and a-six!) Old Fashioneds? Or had Goodman been counting me off, hoping I'd sing? How much Grand Marnier had I snuck while cooking the duck? How much wine at lunch? I needed a drink of water. But ice was ringing against my teeth, and then the table tilted and a punk screamed at me out of Lizzie's t-shirt. T-shirt man gripped a gun-like microphone, his eyes two shot-out holes. He was singing of men and arms, of murderous rage, saying Fuck you, Gramps! Or no, that was Goodman and Sunshine still, trading stories of bad dads and dead pets, pounding an uncertain dactylic hexameter into the tabletop, reciting from the Greek or was it the Greck?
"Tell me the causes now, Muse!"
"Dad, you are *literally* a motherfucking bastard!"
Jump cut. Lizzie again, in medium close-up. Her screaming t-shirt leaning, its angry ghost face fading, her own coming lower now, closer. Then the neon woman must have turned off again, because Lizzie's eyes were shouting at me out of shadows.
What's your story, Betty?
Greck's words? Or no, no—I put my hand on the table lip. "Um… Goodman?" I said, because hadn't he been the one to ask, or maybe answer? Yes, I swear I'd come here to listen to him, to lose myself, and so my other hand was clasping at a sleeve, grasping for something steady as I stood. "Goodman?"

No! Lizzie shook her panicked head—shook the questions from her eyes and replaced them with directives.
Don't make it about him!
Don't make it about them!
Don't make it about good or bad men!
Don't make it about husbands or fathers or grandfathers!
Don't say the same words we've heard all our lives!
But what was I supposed to say—or sing—instead?
O Muse, tell me the causes.
That was when Lizzie Barmaid smashed her tray down on our table. That was when Lizzie Barmaid strobed forward, seemed, almost, to reach out—
"Betty?"
I swear she said my name aloud, yelled it even. And maybe Goodman and Sunshine were pounding out some strange syncopation on the table, no meter I'd ever heard, maybe they were pushing, smash crash, off or back, into some dim distance or paaaaaaghst—but, still, Lizzie Barmaid was looking, and reaching, and calling out my name with thrilling alarm—
Lizzie Barmaid was becoming my spotlight, the rest of the set going dark.
Um, I'm pretty sure you were telling us a story?
How did you even get here?

Erio Piccagliani
Lucia di Lammermoor (featuring Maria Callas), 1954
Gelatin silver print, 14.7 x 10.9 cm / 5.8 x 4.3 in

A
HOW I GOT HERE

I.

She stands in the dark. A spotlight flares, and her eyes flutter shut, her arm floats up, fingers spreading. She has silver skin, silver hair set in shimmering waves, a long silver dress. Bias-cut charmeuse. Hourglass draping. Hidden hook-and-eye closures that line the silken spine. She starts to sing, but I don't know the words.

I know that a whirlwind is a tall column of twirling air. I know that this one spins through a college auditorium, upsetting the audience's careful hair. I know that she opens her mouth and the words blow out in a messy red-gold line until they find him, the man sitting in the second-to-last row. Joe.

The thing is, Lizzie, it doesn't matter which man wrote her words or where. Whether in Italy a century prior ("...spargi un'amara lagrima...!"), or on Tin Pan Alley not so many years before ("...I cried for you...!"), what matters is that the line's light is Joe Flowers's cue, that its touch tumbles him up the center aisle. The audience turns toward him, eyes smiling with surprise, pincurls displaced by the breeze he makes as he taps up the steps to where she stands—our star—the singer—my grandmother. She opens her eyes. Shuts her mouth. He takes her hand. I'm Betty, she should say, but words don't matter here, her words are already whirling away.

Her arm around his neck, his palm light on her back, their two hands lifted, clasped. They are swirling back down the steps and up the aisle and out the double doors, spinning across the starry green, their smiling faces seldom fitting together in the frame. The door to the campus bar opens as they approach, they twirl onto its tiny dance floor. What follows could be a single-take tracking shot—no edits! no cuts!—but for the fact that my grandmother's costume keeps changing. Silver charmeuse turning to silver chiffon, as the camera turns round and round them, as my grandfather turns my grandmother under his arm, her skirt lifting like a slow umbrella. Gray rayon then, embroidered ballerinas pirouetting around the bodice. A white eyelet swing dress, strapless taffeta, little white gloves, big white roses in her hair. The ballroom band shifting from "You'd Be So Nice to Come Home To" to "Nice Work If You Can Get It," my grandfather lowering my grandmother in a dip.

"A Kiss to Build a Dream On." "Until the Real Thing Comes Along." The words don't matter; what matters is that the song spins on, night after starlit, spotlit night. The band plays "Cheek to Cheek," and my grandfather presses his cheek to my grandmother's; it starts on "All the Things You Are," and he whirls her over to the bar. Two Old Fashioneds, please. They lean on the rail and lean into each other, and the band's song fades into the soft story of their future. He will buy her a new house with new things, he whispers, beautiful things for a new beautiful life. He will begin his brilliant career. "I want to be a scientist of sound," he says, even as the strings scoring the scene go quiet. He has an idea, an invention he has only to invent; it came to him during the war, *because* of the war, he—

"I want to work with sound, too." My grandmother laughs, tosses her chin up, the shot cutting off just above her closed lids. Then, as if to counteract the joke she's made of her declaration, she opens her mouth and sings. A high E. Right there at the bar.

My grandfather grabs her wrist. "What are you doing? You'll break the glasses."

2.

He needn't worry. My grandmother has no reason to rage, no reason yet to smash glass. Cut to her daytime face in luminous close-up, eyes shut, a high D, a high C, before her mouth shuts too.

"Now what's come over you?" a voice asks from just beyond the frame. Her singing teacher, Maestro Guardi. "Each time you come here now, you look happier and you sing worse. Tell me, you're in love?"

My grandmother's eyes pop open. "Yes! It's something I never expected! But suddenly it is as if nothing else existed, even my music, which used to mean so much to me."

So tell me of a girl who did not wander, Lizzie. Tell me of a girl who could not claim to be lost, given how easily she achieved all she'd been trained for. The MRS degree, the requisite mister. The gleaming house an hour south of Hollywood, palms leaning all along the lawn. The camera is panning now, past black roses and white rhododendrons, then lingering at a window that reflects the silver dreamgarden we've just left. We dolly past it and, ah—there they are. Grandmother and grandfather, whirling once more, her arm loose around his neck, his light and loving on her back (she wears a gray checked shirtwaist now), through a new house with new, beautiful things. She loves this, doesn't she? The tile that is white as spotlight beneath their feet, the dining table that could pass for a Jens Risom, with its straight, subtle grain, its mean, clean lines—

"I'm so happy," she cries when they reach the living room, the picture window holding them in the center of its frame, sunset filling it, turning them to spinning silhouettes. They dance on, through dusk and starlight, triple step, rock step, kick ball change, dipping at midnight, into morning, until it is hard to tell who is leading, until he's the one turning into her arm, then spinning out, releasing her hand, tapping away toward the foyer.

"Where are you going?" she cries.

His palms are open, fingers splayed. "Work," he sings. Jazz hands, jazz hands, all the way to the door.

"Where?"

"I'm going off to work!" he choruses. And just like that the song stops, she is standing in the dark. Imagine, Lizzie: moments before, she produced a plot merely by closing her eyes, opening her mouth. Now—stillness, silence. It must be a relief when the whirl begins again, my mother taking the quiet house as a cue, starting her swimmy spin around my grandmother's womb. Curling neurotube, metronomic heart. Eyes, nose, mouth, ears, arms. My grandmother raises her own, splays her fingers—jazz hands, jazz hands!—as, inside her, my mother has sudden fingers too. The shirtwaist becomes a muumuu, becomes a loose dressing gown, the belly describing an ever-widening arc, until my grandmother has a new dance partner—one who will cry if she doesn't clutch her close, if she so much as dares to stop spinning.

Now *this* is a cry that could smash glass—a cry that makes the highball in my grandmother's hand tremble, even when the baby, my mother, is in the other room, in the crib at last!—a cry that turns round my grandmother's ear, pleading and unceasing even when her daughter is finally asleep. Nothing helps. Not the pillow over the head, the cotton puffs in the ear. No matter what my grandmother tries, the cry spins on, turning now to a stormy roar, now to distorted music. AABA. A high E, a high D. Hi! Bye! Is the sound becoming a voice then, is the voice beginning to speak?

Bye, it says. Bye-bye! I'm going off to work.

No, that's just Joe, tapping in and out at odd hours—jazz hands! jazz hands!—taking off his gray suit only to put on another, singing a song whose vague words never change, verse verse bridge verse, *work work work*. His silver face zooms toward her. He kisses her, he fades away. My grandmother is left to spin the sirening baby, or to stand alone in the noisiest room.

Sh, she says, *sh sh*. There's no reason to rage. After all, she wanted to work with sound too.

3.

Cut to a hard night at the office then, her dressing table standing in for a desk. Mascara first: clamp once at the lid and again at mid-lash... Blush: smile slightly to find the apples of the cheeks... A mouth appears in the mirror. A red smear: Premier Rouge. At last she pulls on the costume that signals the big number: her loose silver dressing gown, because any opera-writing prodigy or Tin Pan Alley tunesmith can tell you that dishabille draping is timeless. Featherpuff slippers. She totters to the center of the frame. *Sh*, she whispers in the direction of my mother, still wailing in the next room. *I'm going off to work!* Her eyes flutter shut, her arm floats up. *Sh sh*, says the silver shaker, setting her slippers to dance. Brush brush toe heel, kick ball change as she pours a red-gold swirl into her glass. Once she produced a plot merely by opening her mouth, but that story spun out fast, and now she needs more than just her face, the replaceable song, the whirlwind.

She's not young anymore. She's twenty-four. Words didn't matter before, but maybe they do at this late stage? Maybe conforming to the established rhetorical form will conjure a response, the scene partner who can sustain a story far better than a woman alone.

She's a good student, after all, she has that MRS, not to mention a BA in music, she's been studying the librettists (the mad scene is the best scene!), conjugating and declining along with the Tin Pan Alley professionals (*embrace me, embraceable you*), and listening to Joe, too. Yes, she's pretty sure she can give him the answer he wants ("I hear noises"? "Take me in your arms"?), if she just shakes her fingers and opens her mouth and—

"Sh! You're acting hysterical. Now sit down and calm yourself!"

Ah! She got it right then! And even as she resists his description, saying "You must bear with me!"—she feels herself conforming to it. Her voice rising—"You must be gentle with me!"—her face contorting—

"Are you crying?" the scene partner, my grandfather, says. "Why are you crying?"

Doesn't he see? She's just looking sadder, singing better. It's the baby who is crying, through the next night and the next, whirling and twirling in my grandmother's ear at every hour, until it's the next month already—November then March—Saturday, Sunday, Monday—until the sound becomes a voice and the voice begins to speak, the messy whine turning to discernible lines, the shirt is too tight and the light is too bright and the food isn't right, she's on a roll now. Because the mad scene can stay the best scene, and after years of bye-bye lullabies the baby's a little girl.

"I'm going off to work and forget all this!"

"Please don't leave me here all by myself now. I get so frightened when I'm here alone and you go out night after night... Where are you going?"

4.

She finds out eventually. He has to die first. Picture it. The frame careening, my grandfather tearing away from another big bad scene, pressing the gas and making his surroundings fly faster, changing the sound of the very air. His windows are down, the highway a windy, wind-y rush: *shhhhhhhhhhhhhhhhhhhhhhhhhhhhhhhhhhhhhh*! In the sky, the sun soars along with the score, brushes insistent on the snare, *sh sh shhhhhhhhhh*, until—

The supreme hush of the crash.

His obituary was cagey:

Joseph Flowers, an inventor and defense engineer who developed auditory control systems for aircraft and weaponry at the aerospace and defense technology corporation Z—— has died unexpectedly. At the time of his death, Mr. Flowers held nearly seventy-five patents, a number of which were for variations on the technology attending his primary focus, a classified operation rumored to involve a large-scale acoustic suppression apparatus. While failing to offer additional details, Z—— President Frank Mack praised Mr. Flowers's project as one that might yet save millions of lives by dramatically foreshortening future wars.

But there would be declassifications and citations in later years:

Were Flowers's innovations a profound, if subtle, admission not just of the tactical value of belliphonic sound but also its relationship to traumatic memory? Or were they an insidious means of silencing violence, of disabling the public from measuring the effects and costs of war? (Smith, S. *Acoustic Conquest: Sound and Trauma in Wartime.* Text Press, 1991.)

And before that there was the tiny gold key returned with his personal effects, the sheaf of papers my grandmother found in the requisite locked drawer: page after impenetrable page of numbers, notes. But beneath the sheaf—a little leather-bound book, gold leafed, story sized. These pages, my grandmother can understand. She's flipping through them so quickly that the frame wavers. Soon enough, sure enough, a harp sounds and she blurs out. And isn't it a relief to hear him after so long, if only in voiceover? ("The Pacific Theater," my grandfather announces, "June, 1944.") Isn't it a relief to leave the quiet house behind, to find newer (or are they older?) better words?

Isn't it a relief to let him be the hero again, to have any hero at all?

5.

The Pacific Theater. June, 1944.

The beach is already on fire when a mortar shell explodes somewhere close, throwing my grandfather into the air. He lands on soft sand. His eyes shut, he hears nothing but an insane bird singing one long note, a vain avian aria filling his ears. But when he opens his eyes and shakes his head clear, he hears—nothing. And when he struggles up on his elbows, he finds himself within a strange, silent sequence, frame after frame of saturated Technicolor. Clouds of smoke and shrapnel disperse to reveal the bluest sky. Around him, bodies fall beautifully, resting in utter stillness on the red and white sand. To his left, a hand waves its quiet way through blue air—goodbye, goodbye!—before landing on an outcropping of coral. It opens then contracts like a fast blossom. A snail with a shell the size of an infant's fist crawls from beneath the hand and upon the toe of my grandfather's field boot.

The ground is moving, roiling—the flower-hand contracting, the fist-shelled snail slinking, crocodiles creeping alongside them (he will realize only later that these are soldiers, hustling low to the ground)—and yet all is so peaceful, so bright and quiet. Is he dead? He takes a deep breath, his lungs filling with something sweet, a new scent on the breeze. He has forgotten the bougainvillea and hibiscus fringing the beach. He looks up from his field boot, where the snail has snuck forward a centimeter, to see flames quietly blooming. Why has he never noticed that fire smells like flowers?

The next thing he knows, someone is jostling him, and a mouth is an inch from his eyes, shaping the word *down*. Then sound returns, and my grandfather returns to reality. But he will never forget the way that brief obliteration of noise also obliterated fear. He will never forget that it destroyed all thoughts of future and past, delivering the present to him in smells of flowers, in a remote, slow film whose frightening beauty stilled him and filled him with hope.

He will invent a new sort of silencer. A device that will suppress not just the small sounds of guns, but the noisy firing of mortars, rockets... And why stop there? What if there were a way to quiet bombs at the point of detonation? How better to unhinge the enemy? My grandfather grins, the camera cutting to those doomed platoons, weapons at their sides as they gaze dumbly around, discomposed by explosions they can see but never hear.

Before the war, my grandfather studied engineering. Afterward, he goes back to school, studying without cease, breaking only to go to the Music Hall, where he sits in on student concerts or blows a borrowed horn in some practice room until he can no longer hear. His fingers flickering, he sees figures. Cut to the 1908 patent drawing of the first commercial silencer, its dimensions doubling and quintupling as my grandfather plays through the changes: two-five-one, two-five-one. Soon enough he is leaving every day for the low, cement building he refers to only as "work," staying later each night, sketching, testing.

After all, sound deceived him, my grandmother's voice twirling through the auditorium and tricking his ears, those treacly ballads turning barroom to ballroom, turning him round and round the floor until he was dizzy and stupid. "I'm going off to work and forget all this!" He can't stand going home. The living room phonograph is always whirling, my grandfather opening the front door to a fat slow voice spinning out "Love Is Here to Stay." A clarinet twiddles its way down E-flat major, and his wife stumbles unsteadily from the couch, crying, "Are you trying to tell me I'm insane? That's what you think, isn't it? That's what you've been hinting and suggesting for months now, ever since—"

There has to be a way to make it stop. The door to his room is not enough, the pillow over his head is not enough, the cotton puffs in his ears are not enough, and so he begins to work all the time. When his shrill child cries or his wife starts up again ("What *about* my mother? What are you trying to tell me about my mother?"), he practices silencing the sounds he conceives. He never speaks the responses he forms, concentrating instead on the mechanics of their suppression: gauging the pressure of his upper lip against his lower, measuring the angle of his tongue, mentally sketching the set of his jaw—

6.

His methods work for a while.
But then a terrible climax!

7.

His child is what—three, four? Sometimes, when his wife is sleeping off another one, he allows himself to linger at the little girl's door. She wears striped pajamas with a Peter Pan collar, but these are not the details that matter. What matters to her father is her composure. Look at her now, concentrating so intently on her doll! The camera focuses in as she attempts to bend the slim legs, smooth the bright, louche hair. She sits on the carpet. Her mouth is tiny, silent.

But no—no, wait. Suddenly, the girl isn't on the floor. Suddenly, she has flown across the room. She seems to be standing beside the bedside lamp, pulling the doll's blanket over its shade, as if to cover an awful mouth, extinguish a twisted whisper. "Sh," she says, "sh," but what could she possibly hear?

"Fire hazard," the hero yells.

But when he is beside her, when he pulls blanket from shade and lets loose a gust of loud light, she puts her hands on her ears, lips forming the word *no*.

Pan to the hero. We see the fact in his face. "She's passed it onto you."

"Who?" the girl says.

"Your mother. Your mother's mad, Violet."

"Daddy?"

"It began with her imagining things, that she heard noises, footsteps, voices, voices in other people's eyes, and then the voices began to speak to her—"

The little girl begins to back away—her arms float up—does she mean to push him off, or is she asking for comfort? He reaches out, and of course she's crying now, of course her face is—or no—no, wait. She isn't moving, after all—

She isn't crying—

She is—sitting on the carpet as if nothing has happened!?

She inhales, exhales, her mouth a mean line. Her gaze bores through the screen, and I may not have seen *Brutal/Sensitive* yet, but who could forget the climax of that early Greco short, that cult classic, *Sweatpoison*? Jake Rock is Kai Becko this time, and Kai Becko is a boozehound prone to excusable acts of violence that he takes to inexcusable extremes. But you can tell he's tender at heart every time he thinks of his young son, every time he tiptoes through the gruff underbrush to the Airstream where Becko's unstable ex, Bea, keeps the boy. Becko stands on a stack of cinder blocks, peeks through the streaked window, his face going soft as little Timmy plays with his single toy, an overloved bunny named Fluffhead. But what's this? Why is little Timmy's mouth a mean line? Why are his pupils turning purple? Why is he levitating above the shag rug? And why is Frank Sinatra singing "My Way" at inexcusable decibels somewhere offscreen? For twenty-two minutes the film has adhered to a grittily realistic aesthetic logic, but audacity makes an auteur, and Greco has it in spades!

Cut back to the girl, my mother. The famous Violet Flowers, who, at only four years old, still stares, violent eyed, at the camera, my grandfather having faded from the frame. Is she a zombie, like Timmy? She begins, just perceptibly, to shake her head. A demon, then? *Shake shake shake sh sh sh—*

"Sh," she whispers, "stop it," and her staticky gaze holds me still. The camera zooms into extreme close-up, until the screen fills with her noisy eyes, everything she isn't asking me aloud blaring through her glare:

How did you even get here?
Didn't I raise you for something other?
What was up with that sleazy cheesy war scene?
And wherefore the heroine?
You couldn't trust her alone for a single sequence?
You couldn't kill off the hero and stick to it?
Didn't you listen to Lizzie?
Don't talk about fathers or grandfathers!
Don't say the same words we've heard all our lives!

Fine, Mother, fair enough. But are your words really so much better?

8.

The Creation of Violet opened to the public in 199-, and for a little while anyway, my mother was everywhere. Picture her now, on the billboard just before exit 22-C, the actual air blending with the ether she so expertly rendered in azurite. She is lounging, as you already know, Lizzie. Reaching forever into that radical nothing. If it weren't for the tasteful arrangement of text (JUNE 16– JULY 2 ONLY) you and any other schmo with access to the family car might have seen her nipples at a scale not made possible by the fresco itself. And there she is again, aglow in the bus-stop kiosk, or smudging your fingers from the Arts and Leisure pullout, or smiling from the sky at the gaping passengers in the American Airlines ad, her breasts and bush covered this time by an FCC-approved cloud.

Fine, Lizzie—you don't want me to make this about fathers or grandfathers. But what can I bare about my mother that she hasn't already? There she is, again and always, on that *Sunday Magazine* cover, reclining on raw silk, reaching out lackadaisically, her gaze somehow hazier than in the image she painted on her famous ceiling, even though this time it's actually her. The text is placed where it always is, her anatomical expertise—all those sickmaking studies, all that labor over actual cadavers!—be damned. The hot pink lettering bends from her chin to her knees: *Violet Flowers: Where Did She Come From?*

You said it yourself, Lizzie, *The Creation of Violet* changed your life. You probably still have a crick in your neck from staring up, seeking her out amid the silly sybils. I'm sure you were at the opening that June with the other suburban girlteens, stopping for several hours in X before heading off to Hartford for Lilith Fair. And I'm sure you stuck that Sunday cover to so many dorm walls, surer still that you remember nearly every word within.

So you know I didn't invent the loud lampshade. You know that my mother was suffering from a lady's malady before she was even a lady, chronic misophonic migraines that had her draping blankets to quiet the light (the mad scene is the best scene!), that had her father yelling about fire. You know about that father, my grandfather, know he disappeared each day to someplace top secret, until he disappeared for good, just another smash-crash on the highway. You know her great regret, Lizzie: that he flamed away before she found her cure, before she knew that the throbbing, talking light turned to an asset if, and only if, she was painting.

Picture it. My mother at seven or seventeen, standing, *sh sh*, before the canvas. You know already that no matter how poorly she has slept, no matter how giant her head has felt against her tiny grainy pillow, no matter how the moon has strobed at her window, buzzing with loud light, once she wakes and picks up the paintbrush her impairment is no longer an impairment. She sees everything, hears everything—the world spins and shrinks and stops and speaks—but her hypervision does not blur and her hyperhearing does not blare, and my mother is able to lift that brush and answer the world without uttering a single unseemly word.

A scene of eloquent silence, to be sure. But let's not forget, Lizzie, that in the profile proffering it she uttered over three thousand. What more can I add? You even know a bit about her mother, my grandmother, that Friedanian figment turned idle invalid, lobbing her operatic pleas: "I can't bear to think about what I'll do when you're older, oh, what will even be the point? Please don't leave me here all by myself. I get so frightened when I'm here alone. Please, Violet. Promise me!" You remember what my mother promised herself in response. That she would leave no matter what ("School was everything to me! School was my way out!"), that she would never become that kind of woman.

You know, Lizzie, because my mother already said it, already spilled it, already sang. Of a girl trained for dressing tables, dressing gowns, for silver mirrors and silver-skinned heroes. But she was a just girl, a brave girl. A girl who would have been lost if she had not wandered, who would have been x-ed into that distant proto-X for freaking ever if she hadn't exited the house, entered the plane, then arced across the country like a narrative. "Cambridge," my mother announced to the reporter, as if in mythmaking voiceover, "September, 1969." And wasn't it a relief to have a heroine?

3,022 words, to be exact. I still look at my copy of the magazine from time to time, Lizzie, and I'll admit: I have the profile pretty much memorized. What can I say that Violet hasn't?

9.

O tell me of a girl who does not wander! Tell me of a girl who cannot claim to be lost, given that daddy and mommy (yes, *that* mommy) live next door! Tell me of a girl who is not, in fact, a girl any longer, though no one who knows her would object to the term! Tell me of a girl who has no reason to rage—no ostensible, defensible reason, anyway! Tell me of a girl who is not exiled, only x-ed into X for what seems like freaking ever, barely moving beyond her childhood home-porch-lawn to the nearest lawn-porch-home that will have her! O sing of a teak table—is it an actual Jens Risom!?—sing of gleaming, steaming plates of duck à l'orange! Sing of a man's hand cutting the varnish, a man's revoltingly assured and concerted mouth—

Or no—no, wait. Help me, Lizzie. Bar-goddess, daughter of—right, right, that doesn't matter—

For this is not a song of fathers! This is not a song of uncles or granduncles or grandfathers! This is absolutely in no way not even a little bit close to a song of husbands!

Sing not of men then, and sing not of arms. No long labors by land or by sea. Please. Help me find a new beginning.

Our girl is not brave. Our girl is not just. She has not set sail or taken flight, in the car she seems not even to touch the pedal, in the bar she seems not even to order her own drink. Nonetheless, it materializes before her. And she knocks it back like she needs it, like she's suffered dark tempests, razed one city so that she might raise another.

How'd she get here, of all places? She is youngish, for whatever that's worth, undevoted to any mission, undergoing no perilous days, enduring nary a trial. She is no man's son, just Violet's daughter, Betty F.'s granddaughter, some other unrecorded mother's great-great not-so-great-not-so-granddaughter.

    O Lizzie! Invoke thy aid to my unadventurous song!

    Sorry, but our heroine is me, Betty Block, née Bird. And this is my epic of passivity.

10.

Where was I?

11.

My mother spent four years on a specially constructed scaffold, reaching her actual arm toward the one she was sealing into the ceiling with pigment and lime. She spent four years sprawled under spandrels, suspended beneath pendentives. As it turns out, it takes a fair amount of time to exactly replicate—but for the famous absence/amendment at the center!—the ceiling of the Sistine Chapel. A fair amount of time to frame your own lolling, sprawling form with every figure endorsed by the sacerdotal monarchy save the white-bearded, white-cloaked, white man who may well have given you life. So, for a while there, my mother was—shall we say?—busy. There were the thousand-plus giornate lost inside the U's new Arts Center, inches from its specially constructed barrel vault. To say nothing of the giorni that preceded the giornate, to say nothing of the mesi upon mesi. To say nothing of the anni apprenticing to Annigoni—maestro and manifesto-autore ("the works of today's avant-garde are the poisoned fruit of a spiritual decadence!"), expert wearer of a mohair ascot. Picture it, Lizzie. My mother roaming Rome, monitoring the maestro's parking meter or dipping the corner of his cornetto in his caffè, so that she might hold it at an exactly specified distance from his distracted mouth as he focuses his attention on the mouth he is carbonizing into a church wall. Or, come evening, downing aperol spritzes with the Vatican's chief conservator, spritzing her discourse with the precise proportion of wit to piety that will enable her to scale that ultimate scaffold and study without cease. Or picture her some years hence in her studio, grinding pigments by hand, dusting her telephone's keypad with Prussian blue again, with chrome yellow or iron oxide, because she has to hire another assistant or fire the assistant after that. There she is in the medical school's gross anatomy lab, touring prosected cadavers, sketch pad and HB pencil at the ready. And there she is, all dressed up in the courthouse, my handsome father at her side. Don't worry, Lizzie, I know you're not here for a meet-cute or love-marriage-baby-carriage. Anyway, they're hitched already. But the Ministry of Cultural Heritage has gotten litigious again, and my father is also her lawyer.

And where was I, where am I, when am I? I am three, four, seven, ten. It is ten, nine, eight p.m., so I am tucked into bed. It is Monday, or some sorry Tuesday. School is everything to me. School was her way and now it is mine, and so I am sitting still at my desk, Wednesday, Thursday, Friday. To school, to sleep, to school. It is September at last, and then, alas, it is June. Eventually it is always June, and I am strapped onto a plane.

12.

Yet again, the camera zooms. Toward a bright white house with a lawn of leaning green palms. Past color-stunned roses and rhododendrons, every shade of pink and purple. Until we linger at a window that reflects the Technicolor dreamgarden we've just left, superimposing it on the room beyond. We take advantage of this dissolve, slip inside. The lights are off, though a TV glows. A silver face, propped on silver pillows, a disembodied hand reaching in from the edge of the frame with a gift of glowing camellias. A ghostly script spells out *The End*, as, across the room—past a bed piled with mussed bedclothes, past piles of dresses and skirts and nightgowns and tights messing the white tiled floor—a mouth appears in a silver mirror.

"Blush," it says. "Then lipstick. No, the Chanel this time. Premier Rouge. It's what Grable wears." And as the mouth fills with color, as the face moves closer to the mirror, we see a woman and that woman is my grandmother.

I pass her the blush, the lipstick. I pass her the eyelash curler, the eyeliner and eyeshadow. Mascara, obviously. I pass her a bejeweled handbag, an angora sweater wound with soft white flowers. She lets me fill my face, she lets me wear her white kid gloves, her fur, a dress so big on me it's a ballgown.

Makeup!

Costumes!

Places!

Watch us rise from the dressing table, and process to her mussed bed. I rearrange the covers, arrange myself upon them. My grandmother presses the button that means Action.

Ac-tion!

But no matter what we wear; no matter the summer, the year; no matter whether we favor black-and-white or Technicolor this season, the scene you'll see is the same. Faces move over our faces. And we stay that way: absolutely still.

All the better for the camera to zoom again, to focus in on me. My name is Betty Bird, and I'm sorry, but where was I? At Grandma Betty's house, summer after summer. Doing what I always do, going where I always go. Sleep, school, sleep. I fall in one film, wake in another; then I make like the dressing table is a desk; I pull a stool up and listen to my lessons.

For example: If you're using a powder foundation, you have to use a powder blush.

Or: Smile slightly to find the apples of your cheeks.

Or: Clamp once at the lid and again at mid-lash.

Or: If you're feeling bold, go ahead and coat the lower fringe as well.

Or, on this particular afternoon: *You must think of the future and the love you will find there. You must think of marriage and millionaires. When you are in love it is as if nothing else exists. If you don't marry him, you haven't caught him, he's caught you. Say I hate you, then dissolve into his arms. Love is happiness and happiness is better than art. Men aren't attentive to girls who wear glasses. Forget your singing! Love itself is the music, and you will be ruined if you lose it. The first rule is, gentlemen callers have got to wear a necktie. The second rule is, don't let him leave you alone in the house. All my life ever since I was a little girl, I've always had the same dream...*

Hold tight! Take your happiness!

Fine, Lizzie, fair enough: my grandmother didn't use those words exactly.

13.

It was the last afternoon of that particular summer. We couldn't waste it! So, as my grandmother fell back on the covers, as a curtain fell open on the screen, as Lauren Bacall and Marilyn Monroe and Betty Grable whirled in turn into the frame—*How to Marry a Millionaire*—my grandmother continued to teach.

"Here's how you tell you've found just the right outfit. Look at yourself in the mirror as if you *weren't* yourself. What I mean is, think of someone *specific*, and look at yourself the way *they* would. Like, get into the position—the physical position—you're most likely to be in when they see you."

"When who sees me?" Should I admit to being conversant in her rhetoric?

"There must be some boy in your class!" But then she was laughing. "Can you believe the advice we used to get? I read that in an actual *book*. Things are different now, thankfully." She wrung her hands, approximated the rasp of a more grandmotherly grandmother: "You've been provided so many things I wasn't, dearie!" Then, in her own voice: "Okay, okay, no more of that old talk. The future! The future, the future..." Her mouth twitched—merrily? meanly? "What do you think your husband will do? How do you think you'll meet?" Her mouth stopped. She seemed weirdly serious. "What will he look like, Betty? And what will you *wear*?"

Tall Bacall wore a dark and handsome suit when she met her tall, dark, handsome mate; Monroe a silk blouse that matched her champagne hair when she met her main man on a plane. And Grable's Premier Rouge popped against her snowy pallor—not to mention the snowy set—when she met hers on a mountain in Maine. The film ended with all three married, sucking down milkshakes and collapsing in a swoon on the floor of a greasy spoon, the orchestra swelling, Danny snaring a drumroll through the wall.

Have I mentioned Danny?

I haven't!?

I know, Lizzie, I know. This isn't a song of husbands or fathers or brothers, for that matter, but can I help it if I had one? Can I help it if he went to school and sleep and school beside me, while our mother scaled her scaffold and our father represented her in matters of valuation, intellectual property, and the display of obscene material? Can I help it if, come June, Danny too was buckled fast into the plane?

And can I help it that my brother was in the next room, which was crammed with instruments? Yes, while I had pulled a stool up to my grandmother's dressing table, my brother had pulled his closer to the piano. While I'd studied the swoop of Monroe's cat-eye liner—admiring its congruence with her cat-eye frames—Danny had studied the string bass, the saxophone, and now that unbearable snare.

But as our movie switched off, Danny switched to the triangle—*ting!*—and gloom returned to the room. Afternoon. Black-and-white. My grandmother wiped her mouth with her arm. "Marilyn was especially ridiculous in that one, don't you think? That *whis*per! I know she had a tragic life, and the system didn't help, but good lord. Don't tell your mother you made me watch that one." She picked up my hand. *Ting!* She'd given me the white kid gloves to pair with the film, but she looked at them now as if she'd never seen them. "You should take these off. The coat too." It was real fur, white, with a suede collar and tulip-shaped pockets. She was shaking her head, voice riven with sudden disgust. "This isn't right."

"I—" But what words would console her? *I hate Marilyn Monroe?* (I didn't.) *I won't tell my mother?* (I wouldn't. But *why* wouldn't I, why *shouldn't* I?) Anyway, my grandmother didn't wait for me to finish. *Ting!* She snatched up the t-shirt I'd tossed on the bed while assembling my *How to Marry a Millionaire* ensemble, and marched with it toward the door. Would she toss it into my suitcase, tell me to get packing already, tell me she was glad it was our last—

"Chop chop," she said. "Come on, I know just what we can do to atone." She dropped the t-shirt to the floor. *Ting!* Stopped, yet again at the dressing table. "My opera gloves are in the top drawer. Of course for this one we should really have bustles, hats!" She leaned closer to the mirror, so bold as to coat her lower lashes as well. "Cotton swab, please." *Ting!* "Can you douse it? I'm smudged again."

She did look as if she had two black eyes. And am I right to remember that—as I chop-chopped and hopped to—as my disembodied hand flew across the frame the mirror made—as Danny's spare and eerie score continued—*ting!*—as my grandmother leaned out and in and out again, her expression veering from the bitterest disgust to glittering complicity—I felt disgusted too, and not least by my own collusion? Am I right to remember disappointment mingling with relief when she didn't punish me for aiding and abetting her at the mirror, for settling beside her on the bed? The frame flickered with silver flame. *Gaslight*. "You must think of the future, dear, not the past," a man commanded, and Ingrid Bergman was singing. Her bustle was striped, her voice lilting and light ("...spargi un'amara lagrima...!"), and yet her teacher was not impressed. All summer long he'd dispensed his lessons, but still Ingrid Bergman would not learn. "Now what's come over you?" he asked. "Did you never hear your aunt sing? You look like her..."

And did I resemble my own foremother, after all our mutual efforts? I didn't have to look to feel the angry humor on her face. The familiar expression pressing against the dark, one of dismal amusement at her own accountability. An expression that said, Fine, fair enough, I know, I *know*! But I didn't. How did she get here?

Am I right to remember that I snuck my gaze from the screen, began searching the room for clues? Could the scenery tell me the story of this mother, the true terms of the tradition into which I was born? Dresses, skirts, nightgowns, tights, splayed in sad heaps. We'd spent our first week together at the mall, tearing these clothes from their hangers, tossing them to another, plusher floor, Danny bored in the corner. No, Lizzie, no, Guy Greco, I wasn't savvy enough to use the props we bought on those outings to prop up a critique of capitalism, but wasn't I starting to interrogate the desperate waste of our own small system?

How did she get *here*? Tricked out on her back in silk and makeup, as if she were already a corpse? I'd never seen her so much as step into Danny's music room, but did she, when we weren't around? And did she enter the dark room at the end of the hall, lined on every side with books, a behemoth of a desk floating in the middle, gold keyholes in each of its drawers? What was locked inside? What was inside the boxes stacked in the garage, each neatly labeled with a year? 1949. 1969. 1986. Though the headlights swept them whenever we drove off to our dressing rooms, I'd only asked about the painting that hung on the pegboard above, its grand gilt frame itself framed by hammers, a saw. A figure standing in the dark: eyes shut, an arm floating up, fingers spreading. "Is that you?"

"Your grandfather commissioned it. To 'commemorate the night we met.' Obviously such fine art deserves pride of place! Though I do adore the hacksaw. Anyway, yes, it's me, Betty, your namesake, at the most consequential moment of my life, according to your grandpa! It actually was supposed to be a big one. Senior Recital. I was singing."

I see it then, the odd red-gold swirl pouring from the open mouth, the song itself made visible, a messy line.

"*Singing*," she repeated, as if correcting me, "not just gaping, as that awful picture would have it. And thus commenced our whirlwind ro-mahnce."

So I had an image. And I had that word, *whirlwind*. But surely I am right in remembering an immediate need to probe beyond these two tepid clues, to seek out something bigger, stranger, the true and terrible tale I could one day tell my table at the Lonesome? Surely I kept asking that central question, *how did she get here?* Surely the line kept chiming in my mind, kept me from hearing the silly words coming from the silver screen, Ingrid Bergman babbling, "I don't sing like her, I know. I haven't the voice," her teacher correcting, "The trouble is not in your voice alone. Your heart is not in your singing anymore. Each time you come here now, you look happier and you sing worse. Tell me, Paula, you're in love?"

"Yes," Bergman burbled. And, no, Lizzie, no, I'm sorry, but I'm not remembering this right.

I don't want to say the same words we've heard all our lives. But the thing is, I listened to those words ("Love! It's something I never expected!"), and I liked them.

So, no, I didn't resist or interrogate, didn't search that long-gone room, didn't turn to my grandmother and ask for her unrecorded story, because ~~Ingrid Bergman~~ my grandmother was already giving me the answer I wanted, "But suddenly it is as if nothing else existed, even my music, which used to mean so much to me…"

~~Ingrid Bergman's~~ My grandmother's teacher was kind; he knew hers was a rare feeling; she shouldn't waste it. "Now there is a chance to forget tragedy, my child," he whispered. "Take it. Forget your singing too for a while. Happiness is better than art! Free yourself from the past!"

I did my best to obey. I had an image, a word, and now I had ~~Ingrid Bergman~~ my grandmother, adjusting her sporty straw boater. Why ask how she had gotten here when I could see it, when ~~Ingrid Bergman~~ my grandmother was sitting still inside a speeding train? A disembodied hand flew across the frame the window made, but the image did not unsettle me. For the hand belonged to ~~Charles Boyer~~ my grandfather, and wasn't it a relief to have a hero here at last, to have finally found an easy, pleasing path?

"It's all dead in here. The whole place seems to smell of death," ~~Ingrid Bergman~~ my grandmother said, crossing their shared threshold, wrinkling her nose.

"Suppose we make it a new house with new things, beautiful things for a new beautiful life?" ~~Charles Boyer~~ my grandfather offered, and, yes, I let him block out this old house, the odder life it might have proven. ~~Ingrid Bergman~~ My grandmother was dancing around her disordered living room. "I'm so happy," she cried out unhappily. She was spinning, leaning against the piano, bracing herself for chaos or climax. Then she was sitting still beside ~~Charles Boyer~~ my grandfather in a concert hall, face wavering from terror to despair, the face of someone in a car chase or car crash, and ~~Charles Boyer~~ my grandfather was parting the whispering crowd, supporting ~~Ingrid Bergman's~~ my grandmother's elbow, escorting her from the concert hall, as if concerned for her health. ~~Ingrid Bergman~~ My grandmother did seem tired as she dropped onto the silken stool in her dressing room...

"You must be gentle with me. You must bear with me..."

"I'm going out to work and forget all this..."

"No. Please don't leave me here all by myself now. I get so frightened when I am here alone and you go out night after night... I'm frightened of the house. I hear noises ..." *Ting!* "Please don't leave me! Stay with me! Take me in your arms, please!"

~~Charles Boyer~~ My grandfather abandoned the screen, but ~~Ingrid Bergman~~ my grandmother still wore her white silk—opera gloves, roses in her hair. She shifted on a fainting couch, staring at the shifting light. Next to me, my namesake shifted, coughed. The woman onscreen coughed back, sat up. The silent scene seemed to be going on forever, the silver woman standing, pacing, staring in terror at the gaslights. On our floor, heaped clothes whispered reprimands. Outside, drizzle mizzed from dim palms. When I turned from the TV to look at my grandmother, she was looking right back.

Could she see the silly story I'd assigned her skulking around my face?

And what was I afraid of?

That she'd tell me everything I imagined was true?

Sorry, Lizzie. I was afraid she'd tell me it wasn't.

"Was your wedding dress sort of like that?" *Where do you think you'll meet? What will he look like? What will you wear?* I braced myself for her laughter. But would I be embarrassed by its girlish pleasure or by its scorn?

"I got married in City Hall. In black! A business suit, really." She wasn't laughing, just looking past the screen, crying out. ~~My grandfather~~ Charles Boyer was telling ~~my grandmother~~ Ingrid Bergman that her nervous fantasies had been passed down from her mother ("It began with her imagining things, that she heard noises, footsteps, voices, and then the voices began to speak to her.

And in the end, she died in an asylum with no brain at all!"), but my grandmother was looking at something—someone?—beyond him—

"Come join us!"

Danny climbed up on the bed and sat beside me, offered me a bite of his Snickers bar. I declined, and he let the wrapper sail down to the tile. "We were talking about our grandfather," I said, even though we weren't.

"The patents?" he asked. Then he turned to our grandmother, unabashed. "Can you start over? I want to hear it, too."

"The Pacific Theater," she said, "1944."

Or maybe not those words exactly.

14.

O clever man! O sack of Troy or the Pacific Theater, whatever that means! O shield and helmet and rocket and trident and field boot and flak jacket and mortar shell and sopping oar snapped in two! O wine-dark sea! O brinesoaked body! ~~My grandmother's~~ Ingrid Bergman's flinch was frozen on the screen, ~~my grandfather's~~ Charles Boyer's hand ever on her arm, but my brother's smile was widening with each new-old detail, each segment of that scene for which singing was invented. So blame my pandering grandmother, Lizzie, at least a little. However complicit I was in that messy game of make-believe or dress-up, in those weeks of lying quiet inside the house, the beautiful battle scene was all her. And didn't Violet Flowers raise me for something better?

The thing is, Lizzie, I know the story you want to hear about my mother. But I'm afraid I'm going to have to tell you another.

15.

Violet Flowers: Where Did She Come From?

You may not recall its every word, but I know no small portion of the *Sunday Magazine* profile is unforgettable. My mother's description of the way the rain once fell through her migraine: drops long as sewing needles, clattering on the ground as one, yet each stitching the air singly, sewing her into a square of sidewalk. Or her disconcertingly dispassionate description of the uterus she observed in the anatomy lab ("The exterior of the cervix is almost exactly the color of crushed lapis lazuli...") before she decided not just to dispense with the fresco's god figure but also with his "uterine mantle." Or the first, and flashier, pull quote, "Fuck Michelangelo! Seriously, fuck that guy!"

No? Fair enough. But you cannot claim ignorance of the following, famed exchange:

REPORTER: But why *The Creation of Adam*? The opportunity for subversion there is obvious, but did something about it speak directly to *you*, Violet Flowers? You had to spend so much time studying the image, living in it, whatever the broader context! I mean, the hatred—the maniacal hatred—is clear, and very powerful, I might add, but I'm wondering, was there some sort of love there too?

MOM: There was a lot of love.

REPORTER: Tell me more.

MOM: It was all about love.

REPORTER: What do you mean?

MOM: I mean (*sighs, rolls eyes*), I met a boy. The whole thing was for him.

REPORTER: You...met a boy?

MOM: (*laughing, throwing hands up*) I met a boy!

The reporter was twenty-five years my mother's senior. Type his name into your screen and you'll see white upon white upon white: the flippy hair, the flippant grin, the hand-stitched summer-colored suits. He is best known for an *Esquire* piece published in the early seventies in which he elicited not just thousands of words but also several actual tears from a famously laconic, and supposedly stoic, heavyweight champion. But in the course of the several sessions that resulted in *Violet Flowers: Where Did She Come From?* my mother shed not one.

She laughed!

She threw her hands up!

She met a boy!

Picture the exclamation: pulled out, pinkened, and blown up into 72 pt. Picture it superimposed upon the photo that just missed making the cover: my mother, caught seemingly unawares, raw silk wrapped defensively around the famed anatomy, mouth in a mean, pleased twist, eyes cast down and to the side. She looks to be looking right at that pull quote:

"I met a boy!"

It is a look of open contempt, a look that utterly undermines any collaboration with the reporter, a look that reveals all collusion as playacting and thereby makes her failure to collude totally clear, a look that made her retrograde words radical, a look she would adopt again and again in future publicity materials and profiles, the same profiles and materials in which she adopted words like *invisible transhistorical feminist aesthetics* and *hyperperformance as a means toward gender nihilism*, a look you probably felt upon you, Lizzie, as you lay in your dorm bed, Sleater-Kinney blasting, sad magazine scraps shivering on your cinder-block wall.

But the thing is, Lizzie, the words were true. She met a boy. The whole thing was for him.

16.

Cambridge. September, 1969.

My mother may have escaped her own mother, but that doesn't mean she's escaped the flare in the eye, the horrible blare in the ear. Bright, frightening noise is everywhere, in the echoey lecture hall, where two hundred pencils scribble simultaneously; in the enormous dining hall, where five hundred mouths chew simultaneously; and especially in her dorm room, where her desk lamp and the one in the window opposite her own are always, *always* fwumping on simultaneously, singing some buzzy, fuzzy, simultaneous song. Can whoever lives in the offending room hear the loud light too? Or is she the only one so sick?

My mother has come to the university to produce shapes, forms, and lines according to the proper principles; to generate ideas about color, value, texture, and space. Only to find no time for creation, energy only for refutation. And refutation requires just as much concentration as production. Really, she is always, always concentrating, her head aching from the effort it takes to reject, rebuff, renounce, refuse, to keep the lecture-hall scrabbling, the dining-hall grinding, and especially the dorm-room flick-fwumping from filling and stilling her skull.

She turns her light on. Fwump. She shuts her eyes: no. When she sits at her desk the offending window is behind her, and before my mother settled down to study, she checked her own dark view. The window opposite was unlit, she's sure, it was the dullest rectangle, it was a dim empty frame, but now, flick-fwump, she can hear its little distant lamp, now, oh no, she can feel something hot bumping her nape, bright fingers pulling at each hair on the back of her head. No. *No.* She won't open her eyes yet. And when she does, she won't turn around. She puts her hands over her ears. A buzzy fuzz fills them anyway. She presses. Squeezes. No.

No to this latest misophonic migraine. No to frilly feminine frailty. No to fwump and bump, no to flare, no to blare, until finally, one odd hot night in October, all those nos—all that nothing—it's too much.

She turns on the light. She should shut her eyes, should keep the bright sound out, but no—no, this time, she doesn't. She certainly shouldn't turn and look right at it, but she does. The window was black a moment ago, she's certain, but now it blazes, and—in spite of the instructions she is still silently giving herself, in spite of every habitual, ineffectual no—she is scrambling up, pushing off from her desk and across the room, tearing across it, tearing her hair, maybe? Is she rending her garments like some doomed gothic ingénue, flailing like some madwoman across a moor? Is she running at the window as if to throw herself through it?

Yes!

But then—

See what she sees, Lizzie, I dare you. The window across the way no longer a dull rectangle, no longer a dim, empty frame. Picture the face. Picture the hair. (What does he look like? What does he wear?) Picture a posture better suited for Renaissance portraiture.

He stands still as paint, filling the frame to half-length. He is looking at her, maybe, and at first my mother looks back, but then her gaze slides down the line of his right arm, across his clasped hands to the left, until they have ascended the other arm to the eyes. Then down again, up again, to the eyes, the eyes, where light and shadow meet. He is looking at her, isn't he?—or no, maybe not? His chin tilts, he might be glancing just to her right, at some other window even. Her heart trips at the thought even as it permits her to lean closer, to take in all that she can make out of his face from this distance—the soft contours around the mouth—is he smiling?—the muted sfumato tonality. But what transfixes my mother most is his stillness, and the absolute silence that results. She has been looking straight at him for—how long?—and not one noisy motion has disrupted the harmony of his pyramid-shaped pose.

She hasn't noticed the subtle verticals slicing each side of the frame. These are not the thin columns of Mona Lisa's loggia, but university-issued curtains, and my mother doesn't see them at all until they are all she can see. He closes them in one fluid motion, and my mother moves just as smoothly.

Does she know what she's doing? Does she know where she's going? Yes. Will she slam into the stairwell, take the steps two at a time? Yes, yes. Will she cross the wet grass in bare feet? Yes. Will she manage to enter the building opposite, which should be locked at this hour? Yes, she knows she will even before she sees the gold spill on the grass, the door swinging open, three boys in Nehru jackets tumbling out, laughing, the last holding the door for her as if she has every right. Going in? Yes please, yes thank you. Yes, yes, yes. Is the stairwell where she expects it to be? Yes. She has never been inside this dorm, has no official access, never thought to enter it before tonight, but, yes, the layout adheres to her rapid mental map almost exactly, and she is scaling the stairs without hesitation, tumbling out onto the floor opposite her own, where, yes—there—she sees it—the echoing gold spill, that fall of quiet light from the doorway midway down the hall. Is it his? Yes.

She stands in a frame. She sees a bed, neatly made, a blanket folded at the foot. She sees a bedside table, a dresser, a full bookshelf, every spine aligned. She sees a desk pushed against a curtained window. She sees a seated figure, a bent neck, hair that blends in with the lamplight. She sees a boy and that boy is my father.

She looks at him, then feels her gaze pulled up and to the side. On the wall just beside the window, two muscular male figures twist toward each other, and their fingers almost touch.

17.

My mother has come to the university to create, and finally she *is*: fashioning clean, productive days out of the mess of the dead early mornings, when she forces herself awake, the bright room buzzing, forces herself up and into costumes that turn her to somebody new. In a minidress and skinny belt, an Isadora Duncan scarf streaming from her neck, she walks through screaming sunlight to the Art Department, blocks the beaming static with thought. Her head thrumming because there is too much to remember—not about the boy (she knows little at this point but that he stays up late, gets up late, fills his trash bin with Black Jack Taffy wrappers), but about the two boys on his wall, and about the boy who created them.

Fuck Michelangelo! Seriously, fuck that guy! Fuck the flayed human bodies he drew from because where is my mother supposed to find those? Fuck his fondness for naturally milled red chalk, for pens fashioned from sharpened feathers! Fuck the fact that he burned maybe 190,000 of his studies, for fear that his gauche labor be found out! Fuck that, because my mother has found every available facsimile, and she can see them even as she walks. *Bent left leg and bent left arm. Aeneas with Ascanius summoned to leave Dido. Headless figure striding to the right.* The light is all cheerful clatter and her vision clutters the way that fucking guy's sketches did, a foot kicking up from a man's skull, an angel's hair transmuting to a toe. *A man abducting a woman. Left arm and shoulder seen from the back. Male nude turning to the left, male nude turning to the right, male nude turning—*

But then my mother turns the knob, my mother steps inside, and the sound stops and the sun stops and the master's studies at last subside, because my mother is producing her own. She is staring for long quiet hours at her anterior forearm, following the ulna to the lunate, studying each metacarpophalangeal joint. She is outlining, hatching, crosshatching. She is reaching into that radical nothing, until she is reaching across the brick that abuts the famous gate, and reaching for the bronze foot of the founder from the granite plinth below, and reaching her way up thirty limestone steps to the library, reaching, reaching, hello, hello, she knows my father studies on level B. But it isn't until she reaches the ceiling just above his favorite carrel that she knows he has to have seen her. By this time, she is more than just a hand, an arm, a shoulder. By this time, she is also a breast. She is also a chin and a cheek. On the dining hall ceiling above his favored table, she is a stomach, a winking navel. And by the time she hovers above him at night, staring down from the ceiling of his dorm room, she is in the bed below, staring up at herself, at cheek and chin and breast and waist and thigh, at blondish hair and longing eye.

She isn't happy with the ear until she's talked her way into the gross anatomy lab (one of my father's hallmates is pre-med), until she's painted it onto each of the law school's Richardsonian Romanesque arches as well as the boathouse dock. She knows now that my father's name is Jack Bird, that he hails from a suburb twenty minutes west, that he studies history, that he likes to fold his pillow in half while he sleeps, likes her to fold herself, fetal, against him. Still, she can't stop reaching, her arm moving starward on an observatory pilaster or up the trunk of one of the catalpas in the yard. She never reveals to anyone, not to the reporter famed for eliciting crying confessions, not to Danny or me, how she manages these acts of courtship/vandalism without getting caught red-handed—or should I say cadmium-yellow-handed, titanium-white-handed? Her likeness is unmistakable, however. Her expulsion from the university, therefore, inevitable. Even my father objects when she sets her abstract, and then representational, eyes on the gothic vault of the transept dedicated to the Union dead, but not only does he transfer to another school in solidarity, he switches from history to prelaw, so that he might defend her from future legal exposure, so that he might, at the height of the publicity brought by the countersuit, negotiate the terms of the commission from their alma mater's archrival, the commission that will become *The Creation of Violet*, the commission that will change your life, Lizzie.

"He followed me, Betty. Can you believe it? He devoted himself to me utterly!"

Picture my parents then, as I did, eyes aligned, staring up at his 200 square-foot ceiling as it doubles, triples, until it is the 12,000 square-foot flattened barrel vault that will grace the U's new Arts Center. In the year after the opening, my bereft mother seldom got out of bed—the best was behind her, she said—so picture me, too, Lizzie, folding myself in beside her, listening to her talk about the past, letting her turn it to the future.

"Work can be just *every*thing," she said, fingers moving through my hair. "And then, after all that, it's...inert. What's left are the people who love you." She sighed, stared at the empty ceiling above her marriage bed. "Who do you think your great love will be, Betty? You have to find someone who worships you. That's the key, that's the absolute key. What will he look like?"

(And what would I wear?)

"Come on. How do you picture it? How will you meet?"

Madeline McDonnell
Gentle Music (LC & AC on MCM Table), 2024
iPhone photo, 7.6 x 8.9 cm / 3 x 3.5 in

A
HOW I GOT HERE

I.

Cut to the door of my own dorm room, swinging open for the very first time. I have been awaiting this cue, and already I am running, flinging my desperate body toward the window. What will he look like? What will he wear? What dear if narrow destiny will he bear?

He looks like a brick wall, Lizzie. A rusted dumpster. He looks like a red-eyed rat. Lizzie Barmaid, he doesn't look back.

But someone does. I feel eyes like a hand at my nape, eyes tugging each of the hairs on the back of my stupid head. "What are you looking at?"

Speaking of hair, hers was blondish, for whatever that's worth. Longish. She flipped it as I turned—all the better to see the fated face. It was a face like a pastry, round and pallid and mild—a sweet face—a prosperous, unprotected face—a face that was not unlike—my face? I saw big, round eyes that were narrowing, a nose that was scrunching as if to push its pertness away, a flowerbud mouth that was blooming then wilting in dismay. I saw a girl and that girl was—

"Elizabeth?" we said.

"Betty," I answered.

"E," she corrected. "*E*."

Other faces then, filling the doorway. Other voices. "Why would they put two Elizabeths together?" Jenny Oeuf was eyeing the construction-paper flowers taped to our door, markered with our monikers. She turned. "You two even look alike!"

"Seriously..." Calliope Pandey was standing just behind Jenny. "*Single White Female* much?"

Sarah Smalls, who was standing just behind Calliope, let out the bell-like laugh that would fill a multitude of multiplexes a few years hence.

E looked at me. I looked back. Say what you will about our physical resemblance, our common if cast-off first name. We had the same enemies, at least.

2.

Her full name was Elizabeth Leonora Lane. She had come to X from our nation's capital.

"Cool," I said.

"Yeah, super-cool. If you're into phallic monuments built on the backs of slaves."

Her father was an environmental lawyer.

"Cool?" I said.

"Definitely! If you own an oil rig that's just exploded on a couple thousand sea birds." E smiled. "What's your story, anyway? Who'd your family exploit to pay your way in?"

Well, I told her, my father was also a lawyer. But to speak of my father was to speak of his most famous client, and the client herself had told me I might want to lead with something else. She would have been lost if she had not wandered, and now it was my chance to find my own way. And I had done it! I had wandered six whole blocks south! Even E seemed to think I had a story.

So I tried one. The Pacific Theater, 1944. Patents, I said, I guess?

"Whoa," E said. "That's, like, incredibly fucked up."

Yeah, I said, something odd crawling around my face. Pride? Shame?

"Did they ever, like, develop the technology?"

"I don't think so. I mean, I don't really know?"

"Ha! Of course not. All you need to know is that the check clears, right?"

"Right?"

"And 'the Pacific Theater'... I mean, what the fuck is that? Let's irradiate hundreds of thousands of civilians!" E clapped with slow glee, adopted an exaggerated British accent. "Good show! Good show! What a smashing night at the theatre! It's fine as long as they're not white, right?"

"Right?" I repeated. "I mean, not right, I mean—"

"Don't worry, I know what you mean." She lay back on her bed, stuck her bottom lip out, blew up, bangs flying compliantly from her eyes. "My grandfather was in the CIA. And my whole family, like, aestheticizes his torment, or whatever. He lives in this modernist cube in Virginia Beach now, and there's this whole setup. He sits in this $10,000 chair and, like, stares out at the sea, and we're all supposed to be quiet because recruiting Nazi scientists was, like, really hard on Pop-pop."

"Right!" I said.

"It's a five-hour drive, and my mother's busy—like, *incredibly* busy—but she goes there every single Sunday just so she can, like, bring him martinis in his chair. It's ridiculous. I mean, she's the Treasury Secretary's chief of staff."

"Wow!" I said.

"Which is fucked up enough, right?"

"Oh. I mean, right? That must be... Um, it must be an intense job?"

E boinged up into a sitting position. "Exactly! She should be bringing Mr. Secretary his martinis!"

She was wearing a sack dress the color of sand whose primary purpose seemed to be to obscure her body. Still, long hours in dressing rooms had left me with some expertise. I wagered we were the same size. I wasn't wrong. She smoothed the sand, sighed.

"I should cut Deborah some slack, I guess. She was in her twenties when Title IX passed. She couldn't even abort my older brother safely! But it's like, Mom—" E lifted her eyes from the neutral territory of her lap, looked right at me. "I know you were raised for this bullshit, but still. Shouldn't you know better by now?"

The question spread through our shared 200 square feet. It sat there with us.

"My mom's Violet Flowers," I blurted.

E blinked. Tossed her beautiful, obedient hair. "Who?"

3.

She really didn't know, Lizzie. Although she was thinking of majoring in art. "It would make Deborah so fucking crazy. She says I should do whatever I want—"

"Find your own way!"

"Yeah, find my own way, ha ha, but then again who ever regretted getting an MBA? All she cares about is money. I mean, I guess that's what the art world's about too, but at least they don't pretend to be, like, helping people."

I found E's first foray into art-making four months later. I had been studying, sleeping, studying, seldom sparing a moment to look up from my desk, out the window at the so-called world. E had been punctuating outpourings like the first with long periods when she was simply...out. I didn't know where. But then she'd be back in bed, winding her hair around her fingers, telling me about her past, asking after mine. I get it, she said, when I called Violet's hypocrisy *hypocrisy* for the first time. I get it, she said, when I wondered whether Danny had ever lain beside our mother and heard the whole truth, i.e. the deets re: our parents' meet-cute. But where did all this getting it get us? E was there, then she was gone again. I was sleeping, studying, sleeping. One night—morning—afternoon—I really couldn't tell—I stumbled from my bed to E's desk as if I didn't know any better. Little white fists punched the window, punched the face inside it. The campus was covered with snow. I picked up one of E's pencils, put it down, picked up a ring set with a smiling skull, slid it onto my finger. *Single White Female* much? I opened a drawer.

I'd thumbed through half the little black book when I felt my roommate behind me. *Hours Studied/Day: 16, 10, 12, 18, 18, 18, 4 (BAD!). Nights I Closed Down the Library: Sept. 18–27; Oct. 3, 6, 7–15, 18, 20–24. Every night in November (GOOD!). Office Hours Logged, September, October— Grades—Grades—Grades—*

"I'm thinking of calling it *Good Girl*," she said. I turned. Her hair swirled, unperturbed. Her cheeks were rosy from the cold. "Do you think that's too obvious?" There was a sweet, pleading light in her eye: *do you get it?*

"Sorry—" I started. "I was just—" But E didn't let me fail her.

"I'm getting really into conceptual art. Representation's such a lie, no offense to Violet. But then abstraction's so pathetically obsessed with it! Anyway, I figured the piece could start out with obvious stuff, studying, grades. Then it will intensify. Like, I'll list body parts shaved, and paste some actual shavings into the book in really pretty swirly patterns? And then maybe just drop some weird shit into the list, like 'Razor applied to: legs, underarms,' then, like, 'sole of foot, back of ear lobe...' I don't know. I'm still trying to figure out how I can really push it. Like, what's the most abjectly good-girl thing you can think of?"

For a week or so, she was there all the time, explaining, exculpating, brainstorming, picking my good brain. And then suddenly she was going out again, intent on proving her alienation from her material.

"You should come with me tonight. There's this party at Paul and Gio's. They're so pretentious they've forbidden beer, so Aneesh is going to set up some wine pong!"

"You should come with me tonight. There's an actual 'toga rave' at Sigma Chi. I just think we have an anthropological obligation?"

"You should come with me tonight. Ice cream social at the business school! I'm going to drop Deborah's name and make cryptic allusions to an upcoming rate hike."

"You should come with me tonight. There's a No Leather party at Ecology House. You could 'meet a boy'!"

"You should come with me tonight. There's a leather party downtown and they don't check IDs, supposedly. Oh, come on, Betty, please don't make me take Jenny."

But Jenny was already in our doorway, adjusting the too-long leather skirt tall Sarah Smalls had lent her, E whirling around as if caught when she said, "Yeah, Betty, come on. Why are you *always* studying?"

"Didn't you go to convocation, Oeuf?" E laughed like she'd caught Jenny. "*We* are the future! Maybe if Betty studies hard enough there will be, like, a cure for irritable bowel syndrome one day! Or she'll draw upon her deep ancestral understanding of the military industrial complex to broker peace in the Middle East!" E took a ridiculously deep breath, placed her hands on her heart. "I mean, what kind of future are we in for if we don't take our contemporaries seriously?"

"But that's what I'm doing," Jenny insisted. "*Serious*ly, Betty. What are you trying to get?"

E whirled back at me, mouth squirming mirthfully. I could feel my own mouth squirm in return. IBS, we answered, in unison, no cure yet! Myopia. Anorexia. Dysthymia. Carpal tunnel, she said. Social anxiety, I answered. Varicose veins. OCD. The truth was, I wasn't trying to get anything. A migraine, I said, vestibular, misophonic. Unmarried, she said. I'm just trying to be E's art object, I said, offering no further explanation. Good girl! E cried.

I slept, I studied, I slept. This place was supposed to be preparing me for the world, but I seldom had time to look out at it, walk into it. E, on the other hand, started logging long hours at the Media Studies Production Lab, failing to log them in her little black book. She had filmed some of the B-school ice cream social, and she was almost sure there was something *real* in the footage, something, like, scary, and also beautiful, did I get it? When I said solemnly that I did, she laughed. "I'm kidding, obviously. It's such bullshit!" She laughed, but she still left. One night—morning?—afternoon?—I woke to a strange sound. I turned over in bed to see E, turned away in her own bed, shoulders juddering, some strangled song sounding from the clutter of her covers. "Are you crying?" I asked. Her shoulders stilled, she didn't speak. In fact, she didn't speak to me for the next six weeks. Sneaking into her drawer was no big deal, but a direct inquiry?—unforgivable!

Whatever! I got it, or didn't. The truth was, Jenny, Lizzie, whoever, I wasn't trying to get anything. The truth was school was just *every*thing. The way out—or in—or something? Like a good girl, I slept, I studied, I slept.

4.

Then, one morning, I woke up. E's bed was empty, as usual. The wall above it—empty. The fated window was empty, too, sun shining through, my face mercifully erased. I dressed as usual, checked my assignment list as usual, but packed up my books for a change, stepped out into the so-called world.

The sky was enormous, cloudless, Technicolor. Bud-studded branches cut it into frames. I walked along.

I'd made it halfway to the library when a car sailed by, every window down. Violins crescendoed from inside it, something sweet in the swell, repulsive, promising. The next thing I knew I was following the sound. Down Providence Street, missing my turn. Picking up my pace when the music made its own turn on Green. I had a Classics recitation to study for (*if you could only see the dog as he was when Odysseus abandoned him*!), I should have been in the level-B carrel I'd planned to inhabit in homage to my father, but I was racing as if trying to get someplace, some peace, a cure. Running into the future—*we are the future!*—as if that *we* included me, and I was late, or it wasn't too late, or something? As if the violins might cue a mythmaking voiceover ("X, 199-"), roll the film on some decisive scene, the heroine razing the city so that she might raise another. The car swerved left, but I sped right without really knowing why, down a street with the fortuitous name of Spring. Somehow it was April. I pushed without bidding myself to push, opened a heavy door that unmuted new strings. Lightbulbs constellated across a ceiling. An old man blinked at me through glass.

"What's playing?" I was panting like I'd had a near miss.

"Double feature," the man answered. "Douglas Sirk."

Inside the theater, the strings were louder, and the sky was bluer, the color of the water below. I set my backpack on the seat beside me, as Rock Hudson speedboated through the center of the screen.

"Bob!" the girl beside him cried. "Bob, take it easy!"

Hudson threw his head back and laughed. "Easy!? Where's that get ya?"

Rock Hudson was laughing, then he was lying on shore,

hovering near death. He was crying, yelling, laughing again. Only his hair stayed the same.

Jane Wyman's hair was similar. It was Lego hair, removable maybe, but otherwise unchangeable. But Jane changed, sort of. She was sighted and then she was blind. She hated Rock and then she loved him. She slapped his pyroclastic face then twirled into his arms and around an empty ballroom, strings swirling, her skirt lifting like a slow umbrella.

"I'd forgotten how happy I could be," she murmured.

I didn't stay for the second film. I knew I had that Classics recitation (*the women are too careless to take care of him!*). But I exited the theater slowly, lingering through Flick #2's opening credits: *Imitation of Life*. A man sang the titular theme song in the direction of my back, his words mingling in my mind with the final lines of the first feature, so that as I stood under the marquee, blinking, my mind jammed, as ever, with text. *It will obsess you, but it will be a magnificent imitation.* I looked left, then right. *Once you find the way, you'll be bound.*

"Where're you trying to get?" a new voice said.

I looked ahead. A cloud of smoke dissolved and there he was. Boyfriend A.

"Where're you going?" he repeated, a cigarette stuck in his smile.

For once I told the truth. It felt so good I laughed. "I have no idea."

5.

After that, I didn't study and I didn't really sleep. But at least I had answers.

How do you think you'll meet?
What will he look like?
What will you wear?

That spring day before the theater, I wore sweatpants and a ripped-up *Die Harder* t-shirt I'd stolen from my brother. I wore laceless sneakers whose soles detached as I walked, gleefully slapping the ground. My hair divided into crop lines, each yield fertilized with grease.

Boyfriend A didn't mind. He was only nineteen, but his fingers were yellow from smoking. He ran them through my slick hair as if to wipe that sick color off. "You're so dirty," he said.

I really did call him A. His full name, Anaximandros, was too long. I didn't say much else, my speech reduced to a single character. "A," I murmured. "A...A..." Sometimes I said, "Oh, A."

But A talked. He told me he hated this place, the antiseptic classrooms, the antiseptic white button-downs his philosophy professors wore while articulating their antiseptic rhetoric. "Learning's not supposed to be so clean, you know?" A said. "I thought I'd be reading so hard my eyes would bleed!"

I didn't say anything, but A knew I understood. He could see it in my corduroys' stomped-on hems, in my t-shirt's peach-slice pit stains.

"I thought I'd be sleeping with my books! I thought I'd be waking up smeared with them, smelling of them, their ink all over my skin!"

Instead, he was sleeping with me. He had his own room at "the commune," a house shared by thirty weedy-headed upperclassmen on Speen Street. His sheets smelled like yogurt. I fitted myself to him in the fetid darkness, smushed my nose against his spine.

"Ah," A said, contracting into a fetal curl. "This is what intimacy's all about. A return to the infant stage!"

He broke up with me three weeks later. "This is just not what college is all about. Making each other *feel good*... We should be reckoning with some real shit, you know? Love, or whatever, is basically just narcissism."

My punishment for this narcissism was expulsion, my expulsion immediate. The door to A's room opened without my touching it, as if by suction, the landing beyond cupping and puckering. A sat behind me on the bed, his gaze seeming to push me forward, music from other rooms telling the floor to move under my feet. I wasn't telling myself to walk, but I was walking. In the kitchen, empty plates showed me how I looked. My mouth was open, but I didn't speak, my lips two ruby smears. Outside, the sky was also smeared. There was a sunset, and I was walking into it.

It's over, I thought. I caught myself smiling.

In the days that followed, I was distraught, but blissfully so, I was wretched and relieved by my wretchedness. With A, I'd always had to think about what to say (just "A," or the more ambitious and risky "Oh, A"?), but now, at last, I knew. I recited a series of easy lines, confident that any answer suggesting sensation would be correct. (*I'm so* sad. *We were so* happy.) With A, I'd always had to think about what to do—should I move my hips up or down or left or right? Should I keep my mouth open or closed, my tongue sluggish or springy? International peace and medical progress may not have hung in the balance, but how could I consider the bigger picture when the scene I occupied was always a series of close-ups? Should I put my hands on A's cheeks, his shoulder blades, his ass, his back? Who knew? But now, again, *I* did. Mostly, my to-do list contained not-to-dos: eat, sleep, get up, go to class. In place of these actions, I was to lie in bed, staring at the open door until one of the few people I knew appeared in its frame to cue one of the few lines I knew, *I feel so x, I feel so y, I feel*. I was to shift my gaze from Sarah Smalls's (ever-smiling) or E's (increasingly unsmiling), to this or that splotch on the wall, enjoying a keen myopia I would only ever feel again in a bar.

One day, staring at one such splotch, I listened to Patsy Cline repeat herself through my headphones. "I fall," she sang, but her

85

voice was glorious, rising. "To pieces," she added stubbornly, "I fall to pieces," but she didn't sound broken.

6.

I met Boyfriend B at the campus post office. He worked there, behind a lattice of POBs, sliding the mail through. I opened my B the first day of sophomore year in a show of supposed hope—maybe I would see a note from Boyfriend A, I declared to whomever would listen. He would plead unequivocal insanity, he would pledge undying love! Instead, I saw two blue eyes. I stepped back, and it was as if a camera had pulled back, the space around the eyes filling in with additional features: canary hair, tiny ears. B had stepped from behind the POBs; he stood before me, in full frame.

"I didn't mean to startle you. Are you all right?"

B was a bio major, pre-med, he himself hoped to find the cure for any number of ailments one day (IBS, mayhap?), but for now was content conferring diagnoses. I didn't answer his question, but he nodded anyway, taking in the rounded peg of my face, the dress that hung limply below. "Mm-hm," he murmured. The dress was new. I had lost weight since losing A; E said I'd better get some new clothes, didn't I know that's what breakups were good for?

"Mm-hm," B confirmed. I would do.

This is what he needed me to do: spend at least fifteen minutes a day with him, during which time I would perform a series of precise, prescribed motions with my hand. The thing was, he told me, he had this *condition*? Involving, well, an *accretion*...of *fluid*? Did I understand? Did I mind assisting in his treatment? It was so tiresome to attend to himself! He was pursuing medicine out of a passion for helping *others*, didn't I see?

I saw: in B's dark dorm room, I would be required to think even less than I did in my own, where I did little but lie, the same melody making its way across a staff that began at my left ear and ended at my right, scrolling from headphone to headphone, cleaving my brain. "Okay," I said, "sure. I'd love to be of help."

There was no music in B's room. Each day I spent in it sounded the same, looked the same. The bed was white sheeted, its blankets neatly folded at the foot, the area immediately surrounding it prepped as if for surgery. B always lay on his back, nearer to the edge of the bed than the wall; I always sat in a chair, pulled up to the bed as if to a desk, my instruments (a tall bottle of baby oil, three stacked packets of Kleenex) within reach on the nightstand, where they solved the same geometric equation they had the day before. B seldom spoke, but when he did the words came from a preapproved list (1. *faster* 2. *slower* 3. *softer* 4. *harder* 5. *ow* 6. *not yet* 7. *yes* 8. *now*), and he said them in a voice that was clipped and clinical.

"Ow," B said. "Not yet... Yes, now." And yet it was hard to believe my motions could inspire these different reactions, so absolutely alike were they. I knew the procedure I performed was supposed to provide feeling, and yet it was hard to believe feeling possible in that stuck dark room, so numb was my arm. It didn't take me long to realize that, though I didn't want to think, I did still want to feel. This routine was thus all wrong: not only did it prohibit feeling, but it permitted—in the space opened by my sparse surroundings and redundant movements—thinking. I sat in the dark, my hand jerking robotically, thinking of the time that awaited me, a time when I would feel things remembering this place that I'd never felt inside it—wistfulness for the soreness in my wrist, fondness for the bedside table's boring geometry. Why not? What place was better suited for nostalgia than the place where I'd finally imagined a feasible future?

Soon enough, I occupied that future. Soon enough, B had broken up with me. Soon enough, I was thoughtless and feelingful, lying in bed and wandering around campus and pulling aside whatever acquaintances I could find to fill their ears with the same lines. As I spoke, my voice grew strong and sure.

"What now?" I said. "What am I supposed to do now?"

7.

I met Boyfriend C in Nineteenth-Century Architecture. He was a grad student, the TA, and I supposed he'd been picked for the post because he looked like a nineteenth-century architect, his hair gleaming as if Macassared, his mustache two glinting black wings. He was twenty-three. He kept a tin of shoeblack in his breast pocket. I'd see later that his closet was stocked with videos (*Sex-Starved Fuck Sluts #69*, *Great Sexpectations*, *9021-Ho*), but, at first sight of C, I was sure I'd find ribbon ties and top hats.

Meanwhile, the contents of my own closet were shifting. The more I fixed on Boyfriends ABC, the more I was inclined to reinvent the costumes I'd watched while watching movies with my grandmother. Fixated for the moment on C, I fashioned my dress after who else but Ingrid Bergman in *Gaslight*, who seemed to have fashioned hers after the women who flew up out of the darkness of my American Art lectures, their phosphorescent skin blending with their sun-blanched clothes. I wore skirts that fell to the floor in folds, shirts cut low to expose décolletage I hoped C would find both decorous and near-diaphanous, the dark hours in B's bedroom having left me pale. C was, alas, even less impressed than E, who cried, "Jesus, Betty. What kind of future do you want us to be in for? I thought you'd finished your rest cure!" As it turned out, C favored a different sort of classic—*Tits a Wonderful Life*, *Assablanca*—so I soon displayed additional skin. When I met Boyfriend D, I was wearing a ruler-length red skirt with a fuzzy fur trim beneath a smock, a la Vera-Ellen in *White Christmas*; when I met Boyfriend E I was wearing nothing beneath a bedsheet. Boyfriend D was the star of the winter musical, Boyfriend E the star of Visual Art 130, 3-D Foundation, Section F. D pulled me behind the set I was painting, kissed me beneath a smiling wooden moon; E pulled the sheet I'd draped carefully from armpit to ankle, and tied at the waist in the manner of Deborah Kerr as Portia, up; he needed to examine my calves. I was an artist's model that semester; I wore sheets a lot. Soon I was wrapping Boyfriend E's sheets around me before stepping across the hall to the bathroom. Bf E held fast to my foot when I tried to rise, tracing my arch. "This foot is going to be famous," he said. "You can thank me later." When he smiled, his bottom teeth were like bowling pins, skinny and crowded. And when I opened the door, I faced the skinny crowd that always amassed around Bf E's sexiled roommate, impatient for ingress or information.

"What's going on in there, young lady?" the roommate would cry in mock-shock.

8.

Boyfriend E was not to be confused with Girlfriend E. He was not to be confused with my best gossipmate. But E was confused. Anyway, she wanted information. What's going on in there, young lady?

"Come on, girlfriend, you've been working so hard! Are you going to tell me about your latest project?"

"Oh don't worry, girlfriend. You know you'll get all the deets!"

We looked at each other, mouths squirming with—what—hilarity? discomfort? rage?

"Ha!" we said, "ha ha *ha*!"

Hilarity then—good! But was I supposed to say something more? And, if so, what words was I supposed to use?

When you are in love it is as if nothing else exists?
All my life ever since I was a little girl I've always had the same dream?
Boyfriend E really wants a rim job?

"You're seriously not going to tell me anything?" Laughter cracked E's voice in half, but there was something unmoving in her eyes. "What's your fucking problem?"

After all, wasn't our generation of women not just the first born after Title IX, after Roe, but also the first to learn about the G-spot by third grade? *Cunt. Clit. Slut. Slit.* Did I remember a time when I didn't know these words? *Doggy-style! Deepthroating!* So why the smug decorum when faced with the sweet face of my getting-it-mate?

What *was* my fucking problem?

I mean, I wanted this, didn't I? I wanted Boyfriend A to come on my chin, my collarbone, my nose, my ass, my neck, my stomach, my back, the back of my (don't ask) knee. And I wanted Boyfriend B to grab my sticky hand with one of his immaculate own, to turn off the dormitory faucet, to push my nasty fingers toward my nose, whilst instructing me, tonelessly, to smell. Of course I wanted Boyfriend C to flick on *Assablanca*, to tell me this was the beginning of a beautiful slutship as he unhooked the garters he'd just given me, and pushed me down onto my knees. Just as I *wanted* Boyfriends D and E to push my head lapward, to push lips to my ear, and whisper, "What do you want?"

"Tell me what you want! You want this, don't you? Holy shit, you really, really want this," and I did, of course I did.

Hadn't I even asked for it?

I must have. And I must have meant it when I asked—nay, told!—Boyfriend A, or was it B, or was it CDE, to fuck me just like that, hard like that, no, harder, yes, ha-fucking-arder. I must have meant it when I told them to fuck this dumb whore up and down the street, fuck her from behind, fuck her over, fuck her up.

Hurt me, I probably said. Hurt me. Disappointment mingling with relief when I wasn't punished.

Oh, young lady! Oh, Betty, you bad, bad, good, good girl, you

must have wanted it, must have thought of it, asked for it—
Requested it like a favorite song—
Ordered it like an Old Fashioned—

9.

I met Boyfriend F in the dining hall. We stood side by side, swirling soft serve into plastic dishes, though it wasn't even nine a.m. "Poor thing," he said. "Come back to my room and I'll get you a proper meal." He had a half-gallon of mint chocolate chip in his dorm lounge, though we ate it side by side in his bed. "Boyfriend F?" he said after I pushed my lips to his ear, whispered, "What do you want?" Or did he say, "Boyfriend? What the F!?" Either way, he was into guys mostly—he assumed I knew? "I'm happy to cuddle," F said, and I wanted this, holy shit, baby, I really, really motherfucking wanted this after ABCD—after recent unfriendly inquiries made by both Boyfriend and Girlfriend E—oh yes yes fucking *yes* I wanted this break badly. In fact I would do whatever I could to stay inside the warm and undemanding hum of F's arms—I'd eat ice cream at unholy hours, wear the clothes that had won him—a puffy coat over fluffy pajamas—day after day after day. But then Boyfriend F got a boyfriend, and I doffed my pjs, donned proper mourning garb. A black turtleneck, black cigarette pants—cf. Audrey Hepburn in *Funny Face*, though I subbed in strappy heels cast off by Sarah Smalls for Hepburn's black flats. I would be wearing this costume some months later, when those heels had me tripping on a tree root and falling into the magnificently handsome lap of Boyfriend G. Boyfriend G's black clothes matched my own. He had black hair, black-framed glasses. He was holding a black guitar. He broke his A string.

10.

Did I really call him G?
How about My Guy?
Guy Greco, then?
Or just Greck, because, I mean, everyone did?

11.

That's right, Lizzie, I knew Guy Greco, bro-beloved director of *Brutal/Sensitive*. I knew him back when he was seldom Guy, frequently Greck. Though, to me, he was usually just G. I knew him back when his closet was absent of flannel, bereft of lumberjack plaid. I knew him when he was ever black-clad. I knew his cheeks, his chin, his lips, his shoulders, his tongue. I knew him before the famous sideburns, knew that the hair on his chest was splotched in an almost Panda-like pattern, knew that the hair on his dorm floor was never swept up, at least until I came along. I knew that the poster above his bed pledged allegiance not to Truffaut but to my mother's true foe, that it was, I kid you not, Lizzie, the very repro my father had once favored, the famous detail from Fuck-That-Guy's fresco. And I knew G's favorite book, favorite song, favorite team. I knew the relevant lines and lineups, though I'd never so much as flicked on a half-inning of a Mets game, never even heard of Mobb Deep, never read *Ulysses*. But when G asked me would I say yes to say yes my mountain flower, what did I do?

Of course I knew to put my arms around him yes. I knew to draw him down to me so he could feel my breasts all perfume yes and his heart was going like mad and yes I said yes I will Yes.

Yes, I said again, when G asked whether Ventura played third base, and yes, I said, yes, when he inquired whether the one true city was likely to make Prodigy depressed?

Follow-up Q. And when the one-true gets a man such as P, or even G, depressed, what is said man to do?

A. Why, wear a bulletproof vest, of course! If he'd allow me to paraphrase the rhyme in question?

Q. No? Okay then! Why *not* jauntily rap it?

"Are you kidding?" E was the one to offer the A this time. "You rap lines from *The Infamous* to each other? You don't think that's, like, offensive? Not to mention ludicrous?"

To E's point: though G was not a sideburn-touting, conifer-gazing, wannabe auteur as of yet, he was also not a beloved MC raised in the Queensbridge projects. Nope. He was an early graduating high-school valedictorian from Ho-Ho-Kus, whose lily-white body weighed no more than 130 pounds. His love of baseball and hardcore East Coast hip hop notwithstanding, it was hard to picture him holding either bat or gat.

E: "Please tell me you didn't just say *gat*."

"Well, yeah, I mean that's the word Prodigy uses. I should know, I'm supposed to have the whole album memorized by Tuesday. I'm, like, three-quarters of the way there, which is crazy! So many words."

"He gave you an *assignment*?"

Well *that* wasn't the right word. It was more like a project, a group project! And if G had *assigned* it, I knew he'd only done so because...

"Because...?"

Because he...cared...?

"But why do *you* care?" E Q-ed. When I didn't come up with an A right away, she rolled her eyes, rolled toward her splotched cinder block. I figured she'd roll back toward me—I was giving her all the deets, finally, and the variety I knew she'd most relish!—but E didn't get it, or didn't want to get it, or something. Whatever! I did, and I could continue demonstrating my mastery—if not of gastroenterology or geopolitics, then at least of all things G—if only to myself.

Where was I? Oh right: G cared. He cared! About, um, art, and lyricism, and the maintenance of innovative and diverse creative traditions! After all, G himself was a musician, of sorts.

Q. What genre?

A. Ugh. Like, *indie* rock, for lack of a better term. Not that he'd even been able to *play* recently—

Q. Why couldn't he play?

A. Like his boy Stephen Dedalus always said, history was a nightmare from which he was trying to awake, and why was I acting so blithe and dumbly encouraging about his stupid "music," when I *knew*—come on, didn't I?—didn't I *have* to know how complicated it was for him?

I knew that G's professor-father was a pioneer of the minimal music that came to prominence in the mid to late sixties. I knew that said pioneer was most famous—however minimally—for a composition called—minimally: "G." I knew that said composition was composed of tape loops recorded on the G train, rejiggered into the key of G. I knew that—though said tape loops sounded to me like a radiator clanking in the middle of the night—to G they sounded beautiful and painful. As his main man James Joyce might have put it: in that profound ancient male unfamiliar melody G heard the accumulation of the very past!

"Obviously I know!" I said. "My mom's Violet Flowers. The only seat I could find at freshman convocation—" *We are the future!* "—was directly under her naked body."

"I'm sorry." G drew me to him, grimaced his apologies to the Michelangelo above the bed. "I know you get it. At the same time, it's different."

"Different how?" I Q-ed.

"I've heard you on the phone with her. She's, like, a *mom*."

"What do you mean, a *mom*?"

"Betty, this is a good thing. Believe me, you don't want the fucked-up dynamic I have with my dad."

O history! O paternity! O who is the father of any son that any son should love him or he any son, like G's boy Stevie D always said!? I knew the Q tormented poor Bf G. Though his mother (with her weak blood and whey-sour milk!) was the one tormenting him in fact. I'd heard him on the phone too, so I knew. That she was liable to call every night at nine, even though she'd already called thrice in the three hours before. That she was liable to call him "Sweetie Bear," because I heard her doing so no matter how hard he pressed the receiver to his ear. I knew the letters his feet would trace as he paced, said, "I *know*, Mom. I *will*, Mom. I *ahem* love you too"—the ever-expanding Os, the occasional Gs. I knew after listening to but a few one-sided minutes of this colloquy that, back home in Ho-Ho-Kus, his mother was the one to make his bed.

"She makes your bed, doesn't she?"

G grinned disarmingly, and this grin told me he was ashamed and also...not?

Q. Was he even a little bit proud?

Q. Did he think this sad fact somewhat...cute?

Q. Why oh why did I think so too?

I may not have known the answer to that final Q. But I knew what to do.

I made his bed. I stood upon it, restuck a recalcitrant corner of Fuck-That-Guy's fresco to the cinder block. I stacked G's cracked CD cases. I stacked his uncracked books. I neatened his desk, and then I sat down and neatened the half-written draft upon it, correcting spelling, shifting verb phrases into parallel, adding a clarification there, an amplification here and here. Then I held up ~~my~~ his work for G to inspect.

No, I'm not quite sure how I knew to do this.

And I'd stopped offering the juicy, humiliating deets by this time, so I'm not sure how E knew to ask me the following Q: Um, can you please explain why you're being such a fucking *girl*?

12.

I was taking Professor Peltason's Psychoanalytic Approaches to Art that semester; soon enough, it was the only class I was attending. I'd known Prof P since my mother had scaled the scaffold P's department had specially constructed, so I went to every class and even stayed after, collecting the scribbled-over papers my classmates had left behind. *Freud sucks*, they'd written in bubble letters. *Jung swallows*. One such after-class afternoon, Prof P peered at me and kept peering—analytically, near-on psychotically. "Are you all right, Betty?" She touched my cheek. "Your mascara," she said, and I was surprised that she, her two PhDs and 200,000-word vocabulary notwithstanding, could toss off the term, so dry and unadorned were her own eyes. "Oh, honey. It's okay to cry."

Um, duh! I had been crying all morning, all week, all month, crying every time Boyfriend G left me. When he came back we cried together.

"Your mother told me," Prof P said, "and I know you're worried, but I'm sure your grandmother will be all right."

Boyfriend G and I had only been dating two months; we'd broken up seventeen times. No matter!: together, G and I constructed a semantics in which *time* was a meaningless term; together, we made a life that was cyclical and therefore endless. I had loved Boyfriends A through F because being with them meant eventually being without them, and being without them meant not having to act or even aspire, it meant stumbling around campus with headphones plugging my ears, lying in bed with music cleaving my brain, singing without shame. A through F had broken up with me, and I was in mourning.

G broke up with me too, but before I had a chance to don my latest breakup dress (a white chiffon number that made me look particularly consumptive), or to immerse myself in my thoughtless plug-eared performance of mourning/incapacitation, G was unbreaking up with me. "I'm so fucked up," he said, "don't you think? I'm too depressed to be with anyone, but I guess I should try? Otherwise I'd be making depression my master!" We were standing on the main green; I'd made it halfway home before G caught me. He was crying, and, not knowing what else to do, I started crying, too.

So it went. He cried, I cried; I left, he caught me; he left, he came back. G may not have been *the* Guy Greco yet, but he was already an expert in narrative structure. Our story was always at its crash-smash climax, always at its best and worst part, I was always busy mourning what was always being lost. But the best aspect of my arrangement with G was that the life we'd made was cyclical, and yet unpredictable. I knew he would leave me, just as I knew he would come back, but I never knew when. I was therefore helpless in the face of his fancies, and in this perfect helplessness there was perfect liberation. I would never have to decide again; I would only have to wait for G to act, for G's actions to determine my reactions.

"But I'm not acting!" he cried. "I'm helpless, too! There's this thing inside me, this dark, awful thing that controls me. It's like this for all of us. My dad, *obviously*. My grandfather, I'm pretty sure. Making art helps. But only for a while." As it turned out, G's black clothes were no facile stylistic whim; they were *signifiers* of the thing inside him—inside all Greco men! And the black guitar he always carried and never played was a *signifier* of the music the dark thing inside him had silenced. "Or maybe it's your fault," he said. "Usually when I'm, like, *with* someone it makes me want to play. But I don't feel that with you." I had been running my fingers through his black hair—o dear signifier!—but he pushed my hand away and lay back on the bed, the guitar keeping him flat. "Betty," he said, "I've realized something."

"What?"

"You're depressed too. I mean kind of, and I think it's making me worse? So, like, we can still be together, but I don't think we should, you know, *be* together. Whenever we touch it's just like this...infection spreading. You can still sleep here if you want. But we can't sleep in the same bed."

"You only have one bed."

G took off his glasses, wearily rubbed his eyes. "We'll work out the details later, okay? Don't make this harder than it already is."

G said this just before I left for Prof P's seminar, and I was grateful for the cunning timing of his cruelty. Fixating on G, whom I could never lose and was ever losing, meant that if one moment I was walking to class, the next moment class was half-over, and the next moment I was piling my classmates' papers on the lectern, even as Prof P put her hand to my cheek. I was surprised she knew the word *mascara*, maybe, I was surprised to hear her say the word *grandmother*, but I was not surprised by her concerned attention. By this time, I was used to being asked if I was all right.

"She'll be all right," Prof P repeated, "but that doesn't mean it's easy for you."

"Wait," I said. And time obeyed, its swirl slowing. I looked at the wall clock; the red second hand bisected the three. "What did my mother tell you?"

Prof P wore a camel-hair blazer, tan shirt, tan slacks, tan shoes. Her eyes were the same color, a tawny yellow-brown. They blinked. "Just that your grandma had a bit of an accident. But she's stable now, isn't that right?"

"Yes," I said.

Prof P smiled. "Stable," she said again. "Stable! That's a good thing!"

13.

Q. Where was I going?

Q. Why wasn't I ducking into the bathroom opposite P's classroom, slamming into a stall and slapping away my tears?

Q. Why wasn't I stumbling down the stairwell then up the hill and home, all the better to find my mother, cry, "What the fuck?"

Q. Why was I finally not-crying, why was I flying across the bright green and into another dim hallway?

Q. Where was I going, *where was I going*, WHERE WAS I G let me knock for a full minute before he opened the door.

"What are you doing here?" I didn't answer, so he repeated the question.

"My grandmother's in the hospital."

G's mouth unpuckered, his brow unraveled. "Oh," he said. "Oh. I'm sorry."

"Yeah, I think she might be dying?"

"I—god! Fuck! I'm sorry! You're, like, pretty close to her, right?"

"She, like, basically taught me how to live. You know that. I told you that..."

He reached out to me—*sh sh*. "Shit. I mean, I'm really sorry—"

Q. Was there anything—anything at all—Guy Greco could do?

Though this was an unprecedented Q, I knew the A right away. And right away I said it, said words I'd heard in film after film.

"Kiss me!"

Guy Greco did as directed.

14.

When G was in the shower, I called my mother.

"I've been calling *you*," she said. "You're never in your room."

"Whatever! *She's* in the ICU, isn't she? That's what Prof P said. I just stood there like an idiot."

"I'm sorry, sweetie. I—they're probably going to move her today if things continue to— She just—well, she really never should have been driving!" My mother sighed—*shhhhh*. "Anyway, it was scary, but, like Dorothy said, things have improved quite a bit in the last twenty-four hours, and I just—I'm sure she'll be all right."

The window gleamed blackly. Boyfriend G's sheets were scratchy. He turned the shower off. He'd heard me on the phone with my mother before, he could hear me now. And I could feel the drop in my stomach as I fell fully into the narrative. I'd been whisper-yelling when he had the water on, but now my voice grew strong and sure. "She basically taught me how to live, and you don't even tell me?"

"She 'taught you how to live'?" My mother couldn't help but laugh.

Q. Would my grandmother have laughed at my tactics?

A. She was still alive. I could have asked her. But at that moment I wasn't thinking of my grandmother.

15.

It was March and then it was April. Crocuses craned their green necks. The main green gleamed smugly, and I lived in a swirl, no future. G took another shower. I called and called my mother. O history! O maternity! One moment I was talking, the next moment I was yelling, the next I was taking advantage because G was seldom the one to comfort me, the next moment I was kissing, the next moment I was kissing, the next moment I was kissing, the next I was crying, the next I was talking again, the phone sticky against my cheek. My mother's voice was weary, scarily kind. Things had taken a bit of a turn at the hospital. My mother was leaving, but of course she'd come back. "Should I come with you?" I asked. "Oh, sweetie," she said, "I don't think you want to see this." But what did she think I wanted? Silver skin, a soaring score? Was she right? "Things will be all right," I said, "right?" G was strumming an F chord, his inspiration regained. "Will things be all right?" I repeated, waiting for him to pick up my cue, perform his concern already.

It was April somehow. Too warm, and the flowers were riotous. The green was too clean for anyone to die upon it. G and I lay upon it. "But what if I can't be with you now? Like, what even *is* 'now'? Do you think about this shit at all?" He traced my lip, I hoped he wouldn't smudge Grable's favorite. "Do you know they say history 'ended' when we were, like, twelve? Personally, I find that to be kind of a bummer. But I'm grappling with it! Like, if everything is going to be small-scale, can I at least be, like, ethical in relation to the trivial, you know?" Not really, I said, so G put it in simpler terms. Whether or not history had ended, we had. "I know this is, like, a hard time for you and your family, but it wouldn't be *ethical* to stay with you out of pity." So G left, G came back. My mother did and didn't. It was April still. Time was, time was. I was sure there would be more of it. Not just because I wasn't ready for finals. I'd get ready, though, right? Things would be all right?

I stopped showing up to Prof P's seminar. But I began my final paper for the Image and Communication course G and I were both taking that term. My subject? *Untitled Film Stills*, that seminal series of your beloved subject, Lizzie B. Title: "Getting Out from Under 'Plot-riarchy': How Cindy Sherman Unchained Herself from the Chain of Events and Invented a Static Epic." It was April. One moment I was typing, the next moment I was typing, kissing, crying, typing again. A woman was staring at something, or someone, just beyond the frame. She leaned against a wall, her mouth an open trap. A suitcase gawped on her bed, a dog looking on from a stolid pillow—the climactic animal consigned, at last, to needlepoint. My mother hadn't come back. I called her, thinking she might be able to name the framed print in Sherman's photo, some scaled-down warship forced to sail forever across the room's back wall. She didn't answer.

"I don't know," G answered, when I asked what he thought of my thesis statement. "Don't you think this is well-trod ground?" Speaking of which, ours was soft, insolent flowers poking. We lay on it, side by side. "I can't do this now!" G cried. "I have to work!" We lay on his sheets, scritch-scratch. "I can't do this now!" I cried. "I have to work!" Our final paper was due at five. It was April still. And where was my mother? I dropped my paper in the TA's box at 5:03. The wall clock looked stuck even though these things can happen fast. One moment I was looking, the clock was sticking; the next moment it was tocking and I was walking. And far away, a grandmother was doing what grandmothers do. No smash-crash surprises here, apologies, as ever, to Boyfriend G. Who let me knock. Yes, somewhere, cursive was curling across the air, silver letters spelling out *The End*. Knock knock knock knock knock knock knock knock knock. G opened the door at last. I went in, I must have wanted it. I went out, but I promised I'd come back. There was time, still. It was only ten a.m. When had I last been to my room? "Are you okay?" E asked, her first words to me in how long? I was wearing last night's dress. My feet were bare, my face covered in corroded makeup. I looked, no doubt, like I'd spent the night getting punched in the eyes. In truth, I'd spent it crying, and not over my grandmother. Then my father stood in the doorway. "Betty." His tears made me smack my own away. "Betty," he said, "something's happened."

16.

My mother said I didn't want to see it, but that didn't stop me from turning in a charcoal called *Grandmother in (Death)Bed* as my Life Drawing final project (Course description: *Understanding the human figure by direct observation of and drawing from the model*). That didn't stop me from constructing that aforementioned series of dioramas for my Image and Communication final critique. Those boxes-turned-miniature-dressing-rooms, their miniature carpets strewn with miniature clothes. Conspicuously absent? The dolls who might have tried on the dresses and skirts and nightgowns and tights therein. I titled the series *Women in Pain*, then *Goodbyegirlhood*, then *Free Yourself from the Past! (But the Objects Live On)*, then *If She Has Dispensed With Life Can I Now Dispense With Her Lessons?*, then *Death Comes for the Greatest Generation*, which I edited down first to *The Greatest Generation*, and finally to *Death*. Effectual, no? I had a story now, Boyfriend G had as good as said so himself! Though, of course, he said something slightly different during the dioramas' in-class critique.

Two months after my mother flew back to X with my grandmother in a silver box, Boyfriend G flew from X to Aix, where he would spend the summer studying. "I know it's not a great time for you, Betty, but music isn't working for me anymore—it hasn't for a long time, *you* know that. And *Claire's Knee* has changed everything. I think I can figure out my future if I'm closer to Éric?"

Um, sure! What did I care? I was busy with my own story. Boyfriend G may have derided my representation of it ("It's a dressing room. Like, in a mall"), but he'd been awed into submission by the tragic action itself. "Kiss me," I said affectlessly, and he did, he did, he still did, even as he, by which I mean *I*, packed up his most significant signifiers. Black jeans, black t-shirts, black socks, an uncharacteristically bright button-down he'd bought especially for his trip. Sure, wear this shiny lime shirt that doesn't even button up all the way to the collar, G, what do I care? Maybe I stayed in bed for eight days straight upon his departure, but I'd stayed in bed before it too. Maybe I piled his discards on the bedside table—a warped guitar pick, scads of dull black hair, a scrap of paper on which he'd scrawled *song about when dad made me put Fluff-face down, possible title: War?* But that was only because I didn't have anything close at hand to remind me of my grandmother, or myself. When had I last been to this—my—room?

I rolled over in bed. E was kneeling on her own bed, stuffing a gawping suitcase with sand. Sand-colored shift dresses, anyway, sand-colored boots. It was time to pack up what was left of my own things, time to move out of the dorm for one final summer, but—

"Are you still crying?" E asked, not unkindly.

What of it!? I'd cried before, and during, so why not after—why did my tears have to mean that I cared? And, hey, the fact that I wasn't getting out of bed, that I wasn't acting, also meant I was no longer *re*acting! Ha! Look at me, E, and look at me, Lizzie B., failing to seek out the next in the G-designated sequence! No Boyfriend H for me! I was free of G, free of the old questions and costumes, free of my fucking girlhood.

You want proof, Lizzie? Try this: I was no longer following my foremothers' instructions. It was time to find my own way.

17.

Ac-tion!

Ahem.

Aaaaaaaacccccc-*tion!*

And at last I am in desperate, restless motion, smash-crashing through summer and into senior year, into a half-house on Green Street, then out of that half-house to class. "The courtesans and noblewomen of the period have indistinct faces," my Images of Japan's Floating World professor says, "while the men of the theater, particularly those known for female impersonation, are painted with discrete expressions." In my Introduction to Connoisseurship lecture, images move on and off a screen: an open-mouthed shark, caught in a float, inside a formaldehyde-filled box. "Is it art just because an artist made it?" the professor asks. The shark dematerializes, rematerializes, a man in a sharp black crewneck and sharp white crewcut, grinning, sharklike, beside it—the artist, apparently. "But can you call him that?" the professor wonders. The artist or nonartist or con artist disappears, and another man is standing still beside another still box. His hands are buried in the pockets of a bomber jacket, his shoulders stuck in a shrug; the box contains a single vacuum cleaner. "These are the questions we must consider as we consider our curatorial positions," the professor professes. "Can you put a price on a worldview? If so, what is *yours* worth?"

I take his cue—aaaaaaaacccccc-*tion*!—crash-smash out of the classroom, arc up the hill like a plot. Race into the future—I *am* the future!—or at least into Peak Park, an ideal vantage from which to world-view. To stop and stare out at the defunct industrial blocks, the punched-in panes and broken bricks of the factory that made Mary Todd's tea service, the Shah's punch bowl, a 200-some pound tennis trophy, thousands upon thousands of actual silver spoons. To stop and stare at where the clock was knocked from the tower, so that the ghosts can never punch out. Serbian currency! Confederate monuments! To stop and reckon with some real shit. E.g. Can history have ended and also be the nightmare from which we are trying, etc.? But I graduate in eight months, I am in restless, desperate motion, speeding across the overpass that connects Speen to Green, the highway under my feet, in my feet, no time to stop and stare. The maples lining our street reach toward me, branches dancing, leaves spangling green. I graduate in seven months, six, the spangles are red, then gold. At the five count the trees drop their costumes, shimmy in the winter wind, twiggy fingers splayed. Jazz hands, jazz hands! They're going off to work and forget all this! Me too. I will come May, anyway. I will do something, because I've been provided so many things my grandmother wasn't. Or do I mean so many things she was? Anyway, I'll do it. In a-four, in a-three, in a-two.

But first I'll go back to the half-house. To the shower tiled in the pink squares Mamie Eisenhower made popular in the fifties. Wherein I submit to assessing my view—its materials, its condition and attribution, its relative quality—no Boyfriends A–G to curate me! The most adored courtesans of the Edo period had no moles or blemishes on their slender bodies. Through the steam my own body is a freckled cloud, more billow than wisp, but I try not to think about it or feel about it—

After all, E will be here soon, to tell me how I look.

Soon E will come home.

To tell me what to wear, and where to go.

18.

We shared the half-house that year; we shared a foam-spitting couch, a pointless pointillist of a television we named "Georges," after Seurat. We shared swirly glasses of Merlot and Shiraz and Chardonnay, we shared pot after pot of bitter coffee. We shared calm cups of chamomile, but only when we were so hungover that the living room seemed to move at us, the spires of the church next door surging through our windows, panes clanging in time with the bells and brides. Which meant it was Saturday, the week ending like a book, the marriage plot alive and well. We watched it on beveled screens clearer than Georges could ever be, chased our teas with whiskeys, or filled Solo cups to the brim with cheap wine, cheap beer, cheap gin. E was reading Robert Caro's gazillionvolume biography of Lyndon Johnson, and, all through that year, she would chase these weddings with recitations from *The Path to Power* or *Means of Ascent*.

"How's this for a palate cleanser, Betty? Lyndon called his dick 'Jumbo'! He used to wave it around in the Senate bathroom and yell, 'Have you ever seen anything so big?'..."

"He had a really terrible childhood, though. His father would rail at him at the dinner table. 'Goddamn it, Lyndon, you're a failure! You'll be a failure all your life!'..."

"He was so *emotional*, that's what's awesome. He would, like, *cry* about the finer points of legislation. And he was basically assaulting other senators constantly. Grabbing their lapels and, like, pressing his mouth into their ears while he made his case for the jury trial amendment, or whatever..."

Eventually, E would put down the book. "Whaddya say we go out and grab some lapels? Make a deal or two with our fucking contemporaries?"

We'd dress ourselves in the ensembles she assembled, sipping Icehouse from warm cans and leaning into a single mirror, plucking, brushing, drawing—until our faces looked more similar than ever.

"Except you're so pretty," E would say. That's why I needed the spiked belt, her little cousin's shrunken hoodie, her own cubic zirconia cone earrings. My dress had no lapels, so E put her hands on my cheeks. "I mean look at you. You're like a tulip. It's not a problem, but it's a problem, you know? Here, Tulip. This is, like, the worst lipstick ever. It's so ugly it's awesome."

I smeared on the lipstick and looked drunker than I already was, slammed in the mouth with yet another bottle of Merlot. "But now you can't wear it. I mean we can't be those girls, can we?"

"We cannot," E confirmed.

"Well, thanks then, Mr. President. Very altruistic of you. Although, in the Edo period, *small* mouths were idealized."

"Are you holding forth on Japanese culture again? Come on, don't go all Greck on me." E leaned in, blurring my mouth's borders with a Q-tip. Then she stepped back, assessed. "It looks good. Wha-at? You're wondering if your friend Lyndon is a visionary progressive or a scheming opportunist?"

"Or maybe you're just a fucking girl."

"Ha!" E would say. Or: "Was I awful to you about all that?" Or: "I'll be nicer now, I promise, just don't ever leave me like that again!" Or: "Yeah right."

But I *was* right, at least sort of. Under the influence of—what?—the looming future? the dooming winter or blooming spring? half a sixpack of Icehouse?—Elizabeth Leonora-turned-Lyndon Lane had become—if not *such* then at least *sort of*—a fucking girl. How else to explain the fact that E—whose closet was still filled with sandy sacks—now left that closet closed? The fact that she was riffling through mine again?

"I'll trade you my boots!" she said, holding up my spectator pumps. "They're tight on the calves, but they'll change everything if you can take it. You need something commanding! Contrast, tension."

"You don't think I'm tense enough?"

"Come on, Tulip, I'm going to make this worth your while. Do you have that scarf from sophomore year? The morose, diaphanous one?"

"Yeah, and it's functional, too. You can hide your face if you're crying. Bottom drawer, I think? It's not very presidential, though. I mean, what are you, a fucking girl?"

How else to explain the fact that E was riffling through my dresser now, tossing the scarf into a pile that already featured the spectators, a pair of purple fishnets, a pale pink "Marilyn" blouse dotted with hot pink cherries? "Do you still have that filmy white number?" she asked, though she was already shimmying into aquamarine sequins that hugged her hips like Esther Williams's mermaid's tail. "You know, your breakup dress?"

And how else to explain the fact that E, who'd spent the last three-plus years rolling her eyes at the boys in our classes in their big hipster glasses, did not roll her eyes anymore? She held them closed. She covered them with shadow. She held them open, so that she might be so bold as to coat even the lower lashes, so that she might—hours later—stare searingly into the blear of Aneesh's glasses. Or did those chartreuse rims belong to Brad? Oh, who cared, E's reckless laughter seemed to say, why not just be disgusting, why not be depraved by virtue of being anything but, why not just be fucking pretty? It was senior year, it was evening, and when Lyndon Johnson was a kid he used to sit on the fence that bordered his ranch and wait for hours, hoping that just one person would ride by, and so what if E was deigning to talk to that doltish dilettante, Chad Chalke? After all, E'd had four Icehouses and one-quarter of a G&T that was three-quarters tonic. Anyway, they were all the same, these slouchy boys with their slouchless voices. Davey was the one who'd blah-blahed through Futurism: The Shock of the New; Ethan the one who wouldn't stop Theorizing Diaspora. E was wearing a blazer, unborrowed, but neither Farhad nor Gio nor Hari nor Imre nor Jake Rock nor Ken nor Lukas nor Markus nor Nam knew enough to grab her lapels.

They knew anti-globalization and *The Dialogic Imagination*. They knew Dylan, Raekwon, Iverson, Berman, Fanon. They knew what was on the LSAT and MCAT and the Foreign Service exam, knew it didn't matter who was in the White House anyway, they were all shills. Speaking of! They talked McKinsey Merrill Lynch Microsoft, traded interview tips. Come prepared with a significant setback! AmeriCorps. Teach For America. Come prepared with these little blue pills! Could you blame E for giving up, giving in, grabbing Owen's t-shirt mid-gab? Or was that Paul? Green-haired

Paul, skinny as the skinniest third-grader, so tall you had to crane your neck. E was pressing his chest, then lifting her hand from the place where his lapel should have been, letting this selfsame Paul, the Paul whose idiocy almost impressed her it was so epic (or so she'd said when he monopolized our Theories of the Studio section), pin his hand to her suddenly sequined, suddenly permissive ass.

And then E—the same E who'd scoffed at my pitiable fealty to Boyfriend G—that E, aka Lyndon, aka Mr. President—was letting Paul escort her to the bathroom, her head drooping like a tulip. He stooped as he stepped in, and E disappeared behind a door whose cracked panels glowed with pallid light, into a future I never thought she'd find feasible.

And where was I, while E was taking our contemporaries so seriously? I was standing by the folding table at the sad end of the room, finishing a G&T that was three-quarters G. And I was talking to none other than G, who was back in X from Aix, flush with the fabulous future France had unveiled to him.

He was all about film now, he said, and had I seen, oh, of course I probably hadn't *seen* it, but surely I'd at least *heard* of *Heat*, even if neo-noir wasn't my thing, even if I couldn't stomach the viole—

"What the fuck?" G said as I pushed past. "What are you doing?"

"Nothing," I called, gaily. Yet all this nothing was pushing the clock forward, pulling the party apart. I had shoved my way from the folding table to the kitchen, where there was Cider Jack in the fridge, then from the kitchen to the living room, until somehow I was in the bathroom.

E sat on the edge of a rusty tub, her feet crossed at the ankles. "Please tell me that wasn't Greck I saw you talking to."

"Actually, he calls himself 'G. Greco' now?"

"What was up with the Carhartt? I thought he was in Europe, not Wyoming."

"He's changed! Can't you tell? He's given up music. He's devoting himself to les études cinématographiques. What a tool."

"But, I mean, was that the first time? Since his summer in Provence?" E snorted. "Was it, like, okay?"

"It was totally, *totally* fine. We just said What's up."

"Oh, come on! I saw you going all LBJ on him. Paul said you, like, body-checked him!"

"Speaking of Paul, weren't you in here with him? What happened?"

Her eyes flashed with something—hilarity? discomfort? rage? "He wanted to borrow my mascara. Scandalous, right? Are you ready to go? Come on, girlfriend. You look good."

"You know, in the Edo period, women used to blacken and thicken their brows?"

"Why did I wear this scarf?" E asked her reflection. "'Goddamn it, Lyndon! You're a failure. You'll be a failure all your life.' Do you see how insane I look? I hate to say it, but I kind of can't wait until senior year's over. All this fun is so unfun."

"I know. Anyway, I'm ready. Where are we going?"

19.

We were going to The Communist Party, thrown by Jamie #1, who had dressed for the occasion in Stasi gray ("Um, I'm pretty sure that's a Confederate Army jacket?" E said), who had built a wall of Berliner Pfannkuchen across his dining table, not to be torn down until we'd finished 89% of the keg. He blasted Bruce Springsteen at the appointed moment and handed out cans of Coors. Sarah Smalls cried as the wall fell. Jamie #2, who was always borrowing Sarah's bedazzled bustier freshman year, but who now sported a spotty beard, tried to get Sarah to eat one of the mangled jelly donuts. "Doesn't anyone understand that capitalism depends on people's immiseration?" Sarah kept saying, twisting the bright bangles at her wrists.

"Oh my god," E said. "Does she actually get it?"

Sarah seemed to be having a better time at the (Under)Perform Your Gender party a month or two later, though it was hard to tell what level of performance she'd chosen. She wore a lamé sports bra under overalls she'd cinched with an odd, empty toolbelt; the ponytail that emerged from her Red Sox cap seemed to have been flat-ironed then curled. "Oh my god, girl!" she kept saying. "You look amazing!"

"Wait. Does she not get it?" E asked. "Or is she, like, the only one who gets it? Ugh. I'm so tired of this, Tulip. Can we go home and go to sleep and never get up?"

But we didn't go home. And we did get up. And we went to the next party and the next. We went to the Drink Every Time He Says "The Children" party, thrown by the selfsame Sarah Smalls during the State of the Union address. We went to the Miscegenate Wildly! party, thrown by Calliope Pandey ("My fave single white females! Just what this party needed!") as soon as the first crocus bloomed.

But I cite these examples not as evidence of our fun's unfun, but to support the following claim: when E suggested we throw a Betty Got a Job! party I was not put off by the title. Indeed, I was grateful she had not gone in for accuracy—Betty's Mom Got Her a Job! Plus, I knew that, even so softened, the title's derisive cheer would get people—Sarah, Hari, the Jamies, Calliope, Chad Chalke, Jake Rock, and ugh, why not, oh who even gave a shit, Ex-boyfriend G—to come. Maybe I shouldn't have, but I liked the fliers E fashioned, collages of beaming, business-suited Betties: Grable, Cooper, Boop. I liked seeing our party's title next to the titles of lectures on novels or ideologies, my name next to Nader or Shakespeare. I felt grateful to E for putting it there.

We had the Betty's Mom Got Her a Job! party on the penultimate day of that May, the eve of the first morning of my future. We'd graduated only a week before, yet the campus already felt haunted, the weather suddenly unseasonable, our half-house crowded but cold. I stitched my way around the hem of the room, checking windows to make sure they were closed. I talked fuzzily to the few skinny strangers who cried "Betty Got a *Jo-ob!*" when I approached. Ex-Boyfriend G—oh wait, I mean G. Greco—stood, in full flannel at our kitchen table, fiddling with a laptop, wires, a little white box. An isosceles of empty-looking light issued from his hands, images flickering across the wall: an emaciated dog with ribs like spread fingers (Fluff-face?); pink lips against pink ice cream on a cone (who-the-fuck!?). Then hours hadn't passed, but the night had, somehow. People were filing toward the door.

"Betty getting a job is super lame!" someone said.

And then E was whispering in my ear, "We're out of booze."

"Sorry."

"Don't—" *be such a fucking girl* "—apologize. It's not like you drank it."

"I did," I said, "a little? But, um, yeah, I guess I have to get up tomorrow?"

"Why aren't you in bed then? You have a tough day ahead, Tulip. You'll be so busy...what...receiving?"

Betty had gotten a job at the gallery her mother's former assistant had just inherited from his father. According to said mother, the position of receptionist was incontestably important, the gallery's most visible presence. The hire was therefore a profound philosophical decision, as the receptionist's aesthetic had to implicitly express the gallery's "program."

"Totally!" E said. "Which is why you should get some rest! I mean how will you 'implicitly express' on four hours of sleep?

113

It's okay if Sarah and Paul and Jake and Greck stay, right? Paul went to get a couple of six-packs. And you said you're cool with Greck, so...?"

"Of course," I said.

"Great. Okay then, Tulip. Off to bed!"

Was I obeying my commander in chief or calling her bluff? Anyway, I was on my lumpy futon, picturing Jake Rock and Paul and Sarah Smalls sitting on the other side of the wall, twirling their glasses, ice tinking. And, yeah, sure, I pictured Boyfriend G, I mean, Ex-Bf G, why not? And I pictured my beloved Mr. President, lying on her side, head propped on one hand, the other picking debris—blackened pennies, bobby pins—from the wide spaces between the floorboards. At first their voices were soft, trapped animals, but soon I discerned words.

"...maybe hit up the A.T., man. Or do you think the Camino Inca's, like, realer...?"

"...make your own trail, dude! You know, like, couch-surf, beach-sleep. Get a job only when you have to..."

"...um, speaking of jobs, maybe you should be a little quieter? Re*mem*ber? Betty has a reason to get up in the morning—by which I mean a reason to go on living! Unlike us..."

Laughter, the clink of toasts, followed by that inimitable baritone drone. Ugh. Or should I say uGGh? He'd had a revelation in Aix, an artistic and thereby *intrinsically* political insight. Like, what if Éric Rohmer had made *Bloodsport*? And what if G took É's edict to look at thought rather than action by looking at action *as* thought? I put my pillow over my head, pushed it against my ears. But then I pulled it off. Was E actually outlining her own ambitions? "I mean?" she started. "Probably, like, pack? Leave and never come back, something along those lines?"

I was flat on my back in the darkness, but I could see my getting-it-mate's face. And I could feel myself fashioning my own after hers, fastening my features into slackness, until they were inanimate, yet animate with scorn.

"I don't know," she went on, voice as empty as her eyes surely were. "Our nation's capital, I guess?"

"That's awesome!" Sarah said. "You can, like, really make a difference there."

"Whatever," E answered. "Aren't we all just moving back in with our parents?"

20.

But E didn't move back to DC. She didn't move back in with Deborah or Polluter Defender, Esquire. I was the one unable to make rent on my receptionist's salary, the one who slunk back to my parents' once E left her half of the half-house, glorying her way into a glorified closet on Delancey.

Lower East Side—obviously. The one true city—obviously-er.

"That's so...obvious," I said.

"I know." E laughed. "I even have a fire escape. I sit on it and smoke."

"You smoke?"

She called every night the first year of our future. I lay in my childhood bed with the lights off, listening to the one true through the phone—yellow horns, words cresting and fading as strangers passed her on the sidewalk. I could see that brindled sidewalk, streaked by sign light, scattered with glittering shards. "Tulip," E yelled, "can you hear me?"

Yes, sir, loud and clear, sir. Yes, E, I hear you. I get you.

"I'm so sad it's making me sick. Everything's awful."

I didn't believe her. I could see her too well: that neoned hair streaking; her heels nicking pavement, leaving wakes of star pricks; her lipstick gashing the night. She wasn't sad. She was just drunk.

She'd been to a party in a penthouse so high and strange it seemed more like a spaceship floating over the city, or to an opening in an icy room where ruddy paintings hung like carcasses from hooks, or to a dinner in some basement restaurant, the tables too low, the candles like fat, glowing thumbs. She'd been out and she'd had—my god!—three glasses of wine! Two gin and tonics even! I envied E her ability to tumble into drunken distress with a blood-alcohol level equal to the one I reached ten minutes into dinner with my parents.

I was hours past it now. Sure, Betty's Mom Had Gotten Her a Job!, but Betty had also pictured that job as something out of *His Girl Friday*—candlestick telephones clanging, boss and Betty talking over calls and coworkers alike, all so that they might talk over each other.

They're at each other's throats! And in each other's hearts!
He can't work without her! She can't live without him!

The problem? There weren't any candlestick telephones in the gallery, duh. There weren't any coworkers. There weren't even any paintings hanging on the bright, chilly walls. And there certainly weren't sounds to speak over, not unless you counted the diminutive warriors shrieking from Betty's mother's former assistant's giant computer screen. When the behoodied and sad-slouching Solly S. Snodgrass was even there—asking shamefacedly after my *mom*, italics his; making a show of staring at the blank walls and scratching his chin scruff before retreating to the computer to boot up *Orcus vs. Orcas* or *Counter-Counter-Strike*. He usually wasn't.

Which meant that Betty spent her days sitting in her absent boss's chair, staring at his abandoned if beloved monitor, into the infantile internet. Or at the space bequeathed by his birthright—his walls, his windows, wherein, every now and again, she'd spy a face. It was at those moments when she realized she herself must seem an art object, a performance artist or static installation, the single piece (*Betty Got a Job!*) stored within that strange white cube.

Is it any wonder then that Betty lay in bed each night watching the ceiling spin, waiting for word from E?

"What's so awful about it?" I asked her.

"Well, it's a fucked-up time in the world, right?"

"Right!"

"But I feel like the people in this city have *always* been jerks. They're so—well. You get it."

"Totally!"

"They're grasping. And sometimes I'm at these parties or these, like, dinners, and I think about how much I wanted this, how if my younger self could see the future, you know, if she could see me with these rich, grasping people, she'd be happy. I know I talked a good game, but I did want this, I can admit it. And now it's awful."

I made additional sounds of understanding: mms, ahs. I watched moths kamikaze against the windowpanes. My lids drooped and months passed, snow flying at the panes like moths.

"At least you're doing something with your life..." I told and told and told her.

21.

But no matter how wispy I made my voice, no matter how pathetic or bathetic or unsympathetic I made my life, E could starve her own voice to a vicious vacancy; she could whittle her life to the thinnest meanest line.

"Ha! Do you know what I did with my life today? I called in sick this morning because I was. Then I threw up in the trash can because I couldn't make it to the bathroom. Then I was too tired to clean it up, so you know what I did? With my life?"

I made a meager sound of inquiry: an mm? an ah?

"I put the trash can in the closet. And when I had to throw

up again? Luckily, I have two trash cans. Can you guess where I put the second one?"

"I can."

"And then do you know what I did? With my *life*? I went to work. Because it seemed better to be sick there, it's so fucking depressing in this apartment. Also, Regis has, like, thirty trash cans."

Regis was the rephotographer and collagist E worked for that first summer. He was a small bald man who always wore pleated khakis, though he'd been an enfant terrible in the eighties.

"He actually says that. 'Did I mention I was an enfant terrible in the eighties?' He says 'in the eighties'!"

"At least he's around. It's like I foreclosed on Solly's house or something."

"I don't get it, though. Where does he go? And why is he scared of *you*?"

"Violet, I assume. He doesn't want me telling her what a shitshow the whole thing is! Or, I don't know, maybe I'm wrong. Maybe he's off doing important curatorial things? I guess he could be visiting artists' studios? That's what a gallery director's supposed to do, right?"

"How should I know, Tulip?"

"More relevantly, how should I? Do you think he thought I would? Maybe I was, like, his last best hope. God, I don't know… Every time he comes in I'm almost like, It's okay, Solly! I know you don't care about art! I get that you just want to go home and play *State Violence*! It's totally fine, I seriously don't blame you!"

"But what does he expect you to do when he's out gaming? Are the walls still empty?"

"Utterly."

"But has he given you, like, 'work'?"

In fact, Solly had given me one task: to thumb through a thick stack of catalogues stocked with the paintings his dead progenitors had peddled. Windswept seascapes, pallid children, watercolors of woebegone wineglasses. Grandmother stuff, as he called it. He was hoping to become an expert in...the opposite? Could I help him cast off that past?

I thumbed, rethumbed. Inspected vases and lighthouses, blond lovers in bland clinches. Asked the questions I'd been assigned.

What is the opposite of still life?
What is the opposite of romance?
"Nope," I said to E.
What is the opposite of grandmother?
"So what do you do?"
"What do I do with my *life*? Um? There's this thing you may have heard of? It's called the internet?"
"Oh, I get it, Tulip, believe me. You don't even know how I get it. You're lucky, though, you know? I mean, I make less than no money, but at this point I would *pay* to be alone."

No matter the hour, Regis was there, pasting rephotographed photographs of nippleless breasts over rephotographed photographs of legless chairs. He performed said pasting in a giant concrete room that was separated by glass blocks from the giant concrete room in which E did not paste, did not speak. Unless Regis was on the line, that is.

"He's like fifty feet away and he calls me on the *phone*. He needed a receptionist because he's such an important artist, an enfant terrible in the eighties. And he gave me these super intricate instructions about what I'm supposed to say to his Miami dealer as opposed to his LA dealer..." E sighed. "The phone does ring off the hook, but it's always him. He wants a coffee, he says, but he doesn't want a coffee. He wants me to rub his shoulders, can you believe that shit?"

"Do you do it?"

"Ugh. I don't know. I mean, mostly, he just wants to *talk*. It's so fucking sad."

"*Receptionist* is such an awful word. How is this our lives? You promised me a better future, Mr. President!"

22.

But E was not a receptionist for long. By October, she worked as a gallery assistant, attending to what tasks the director—a tinsel-haired anorexic who spent an hour every day consuming a single container of coffee yogurt—did not have time for. "You know how it is. I fill out forms. Conditions reports. Sales reports. I'm not a receptionist anymore, but I am a secretary. Basically."

"What I'd give to fill out a form!"

"Forms shmorms. You run a gallery now, girlfriend."

It was true that Solly had—at short last!—left me in charge. Anyway, he'd left me, appearing one morning sans slouch and hoodie, avec madras shirt and odd smile, only to announce his disappearance. His therapist had prescribed travel. He needed distance, she said, in order to determine if this was the future he desired. His therapist was so awesome, by the way. She reminded him a lot of my mom, actually? *Any*way. With her help he'd made a decision. He was going to this, like, ashram? And, um, did I mind if he sat there for a sec? There was some stuff on the hard drive he, like, needed to copy.

But of course, Solly! However could you show your face at the ashram without *Slaves to Gorestar: Blood Conquest*!?

"I thought I was out of a job," I told E, "but he seems to assume I'll stay? He obviously doesn't think I have anything better to do. And he's right! That's not the worst part, though. I realized something, listening to him. He actually takes himself seriously. Like, he thinks his future really matters, forget what the evidence suggests. *Solly*!"

"But don't you see? Now's the perfect opportunity to show him!

You're the de facto director—directress? Whatever. The point is," E made her voice a movie trailer's, sonorous and grandiose, "you can restore the Snodgrass Gallery to long-lost prominence!"

"Oh totally! My first exhibit's going to take the art world by storm! It'll be a performance installation, just empty white walls and this empty white desk and me, sitting there, googling Sarah Smalls and Calliope Pandey again and again. I'll call it *Betty Got a Job!*"

I laughed as if this fantasy were the ultimate folly, as if I hadn't wasted a moment imagining *Betty Got a Job!* getting the job done, had never ever pictured myself googling pictures of myself googling pictures of myself. But close my eyes and there I was again, framed by the gallery window, and inside every window on Solly's screen, sporting the sort of Chevron fit-and-flare not seen since Rosalind Russell told Cary Grant she was quitting to go someplace where she could be a woman. "*Betty Got a Job!* Takes Art World by Storm!" There I was sitting in Solly's chair, watching myself sitting on some well-lit late-night couch. "So, Betty," the bendy host was crooning, pompadour leaning, "what can you tell me about *Betty Got a Job!*?"

The real question was what would I tell E? How would I break it to Mr. President if I made a breakthrough, even one that took a more ordinary form? Would she forgive me for letting my future fill when hers stayed, defiantly, blank? How would I tell her I'd left her like that again? The thought was horrifying.

It was also immaterial. By this time, I was too busy at night to do anything by day but reminisce re: the previous evening.

Have I mentioned my husband, Lizzie?

Well, let's keep it that way. This is not a song of husbands, after all. But I suppose I might at least admit: by this time, a certain Boyfriend H had stepped onto the soundstage of his biopic, aka his front porch, aka my life.

"He didn't really say ashram, did he?" E asked.

"Who?" *Had* I mentioned him?

"Solly, duh! Oh my god, what an absolute tool."

For the first time all night, her words sounded sincere. And E had a right to her outrage, maybe even more so than I. For Elizabeth Lyndon Lane would never speak of her uncertain future with the unapologetic faith, the unprotected fervor, favored by ashram-goers like Solly S. Snodgrass. She was absolutely abstemious in that regard, so strict in her denial of her own prospects it had become hard to believe she allowed herself to consider them. But did she? I didn't dare ask. No, no matter what her mind dared show her—what exhibits it curated—what reviews, what reactions, what action—E never spoke of her future at all anymore.

23.

She only told me her gallery had closed a month after the fact.

"It was so weird. These men came in, like, uniforms, and said we had a health code violation. Marlene was irate—it was only eleven, she hadn't had her yogurt. She kept stalking around, waving her arms. 'What do you mean *health code*? We're not making burgers here!' She kept saying *burgers, burgers*, and her eyes were, like, lighting up."

"You should come back to X. Just visit so long as you're unemployed. Please? My old stuffed animals won't stop staring at me, and it's freaking me out!" Of course if E visited, she'd have to meet—

"You know who's staring at me? The dude across the airshaft. I was changing the other night and he actually started jerking off. I was too tired to close the blinds. Instead I just lay here, you know, weeping."

"Oh my god," I said. "Come back to X."

But, true to her word, E had left and would never, etc. Which is to say: she had a new job already, and this time even my mother was impressed.

24.

"'Not everyone gets their start at Christie's,' she said."

E sighed. "Tell her I work in the bins."

"The bins?"

"The *bins*, Tulip. I report to this deserted basement. And I stand for hours in these stupid heels because Christie—" yes, E's boss was actually named Christie "—says 'Christie's girls don't wear flats.' She's always making these pronouncements about 'Christie's girls.' Anyway, all I do is measure these awful dusty paintings, the dregs of the dregs of the dregs. And the pay is criminal. Not that I'm *not* disgustingly privileged, but all the other 'bin girls' are, like, eighth-generation trust-funders. At least my great-great-*great* grandfather had to work for it! So, I was talking to one of them in the break room—her name is *also* Krystie, though she spells it with a K and a Y, 'like the jelly.' She actually said that. And I asked her what her parents do because she kept bringing them up, she was calling them Muzzy and Dazzy. So I say, 'What do Muzzy and Dazzy do,' because that's all anyone talks about in this stupid city anyway, and she says, in this really bored voice, 'Oh... they languish.'"

"But that's what I do!"

"Well, we can't all be as lucky as you and Muzzy and Dazzy, I guess."

25.

But E was lucky enough to find her way out of the basement, out of the dregs, onto the nineteenth floor of a 1920s Beaux-Arts building within the year. Seventh Avenue, obviously. Chelsea, obviously-er. She'd been hired as an editorial researcher at *ArtAgora*. She shared a lucite cubicle with a nineteen-year-old named Vladika.

"I'm pretty sure it's some kind of mail-order situation. Stellan likes to keep her close, I guess. I just hope that's where the creepiness ends. She never does anything, but you can't be too hard on her, you know?"

"Ugh."

"Exactly. And guess what my first assignment was? I was going over this article about a Delaunay sale…"

"Sonia or Robert?"

"Who cares? Anyway, I needed to confirm a quote. Guess who I had to call?"

"Christie?"

"K-Y jelly. She was *promoted*. Apparently K-Y speaks fluent Mandarin, which makes her 'a popular contact for the burgeoning Chinese market.'"

"I'm sorry."

"*I'm* sorry. Seriously, tell Violet I am eternally sorry for disappointing her."

"Um, I think my own apology might take precedence? I mean, Betty's mom got her a job! And Betty's mom is, shall we say, a touch displeased with what her daughter's made of the opportunity?"

In fact, I was doing something more with it than retreating to my childhood bed as soon as I came home, watching the ceiling spin, waiting for E to call. Indeed, as far as my not-particularly displeased mother could see, I was nigh-on industrious now, racing up to my room and ransacking my closet, applying the stringent aesthetic standards befitting a rising gallerist to each image that floated in the silver screen my mirror made. I tossed the assemblages that were not up to par on the floor, no time to pick up my dresses and skirts and near-gowns and tights because I was beyond industrious now, I was in desperate restless motion, running back down the stairs. "You need a necklace!" my mother called, but I was too busy to answer, I was rushing out the door and finding my own way, across our lawn, his lawn. *What will you wear? Where will you meet? What will he look like?*

"What does he look like anyway?" E said. "You tell me nothing, young lady!"

I must have mentioned him then.

"Pretty good, thank god. I mean, at least it gives me some excuse! We watched a movie last night and he kept pausing it to provide a critical commentary. You know, like a DVD extra? And when he wasn't doing that he was whispering along with the voiceover."

"Ugh."

"Exactly."

"What movie?"

"*Mr. Arkadin*. Orson Welles. Artifice is, like, his thing."

"So are you going to marry him already? Provide Violet with an heiress?"

"Are you kidding? You'd never forgive me."

"Oh please, Tulip. You know how Deborah's all about 'information-sharing' ever since she left DC for Dot-com-landia? Well, she's been bombarding me as usual. But every article she sends these days is about how reproductive biologists *thought* fertility started to drop off in the early thirties, but actually it's more like twenty-seven, twenty-six? Today's was 'How Becoming a Mom Made Me a Better CEO.' So, anyway, remember Jerkoff across the airshaft? I saw him today on my way to work, and he actually looked okay up close. A little oily, but...alert at least? And I'd *just* gotten off the phone with Deborah, so I almost proposed right there. I want to be a good daughter!"

I didn't believe her. I could see her too well—sunstruck hair streaking, heels nicking pavement—her front stoop, the sidewalk, the steps leading down to the subway. Even as she descended, E looked up, away from the sodden, stomped-upon tabloids (*U.S. Warns: We'll Nuke You! Britney and Justin: Dance Battle!*). She looked at the strip of fluorescence bisecting the ceiling, and when she exited the train, when she rose up from the underground, when she strode down Seventh, her eyes stayed on a dim strip of sky. She entered her building, pressed UP without looking down. And when she ascended past the second to the seventh floor, the seventeenth, the eighteenth, she seemed propelled by her own uptilted head.

"You're probably right," I said. "It's past time to give up on my future. I should totally have a baby!"

"No-o! Giving up is my job. Oh, Tulip, don't you get it? *You* are my only hope!"

26.

In the second year of our future, E hardly called. It wasn't her fault. The truth was I hardly answered, so busy was I next door.

And on those rare nights when I wasn't, I also wasn't sleeping. I lay in my childhood bed and watched the ceiling spin. I contemplated calling E. I waited for her to call me.

She didn't. So—one star-smeared night when Boyfriend H was away at another conference—I dialed.

"Betty!" E's voice was high, strained.

"Is someone there?" Had she mentioned someone? Had I missed it?

"Who? Anyway, you're one to talk. Where's the professor?"

"Oh, he's off professing."

"At one a.m.?"

"At one a.m.!"

The line clicked. Somewhere in my parents' house a clock ticked. "So," I said.

"So."

"How—" we started.

I let E finish. "How are things going with Prof H anyway?"

I gave what answer my getting-it-mate would get. Anyway, it was the truth. "Awful."

E blew a sigh into her mouthpiece—*shhhhhhhh*. "You're still planning on marrying him, though? That's still happening?"

"Yeah, but—"

"So! It can't be that bad, Tulip. Come on, I dare you to tell me one good thing about being with this one."

I watched the ceiling. It spun. I waited for words that would cut her. They didn't come. "I don't know. I mean, I guess I like that I can...say whatever to him? I mean, I'm *good* at being with him? Like, I don't worry about it. I just say stuff." But why was this an achievement? And why was E making me admit something so meager, so mean? What had happened to getting it? "How are things with you?"

"*You* know."

"No."

"No, I guess you don't. Well, all I do is work. And the job, I mean, it's fine? It's not what I want to do forever, obviously, but I don't know. I'm pretty good at it. And I've met some interesting people. There's this one artist, Arnie, he makes these dioramas." Her voice was afflicted by a sudden, sickly sincerity. "Anyway..." She laughed. "I guess what I'm saying is life's not actually that bad?"

"I get it," I said. And I did. E's life had to be better than not-that-bad, it had to be awfully unawful for her to admit so much.

"So things are awful or really great or whatever with the professor? God, I can't believe you're getting married. I wish you'd have a wedding, though. What's this city hall bullshit?"

Oh, I got it. E's life had to be greater than really great for her to speak of the future this way to me, her only hope. "That's cool you're liking your job more," I said. "Sounds like you've got it all figured out. You know, like, 'what is the opposite of still life?'"

"What does that mean?"

"I don't know. It's something Solly used to say."

"What a weirdo. I guess the ashram's working out?"

"They have the internet there, anyway. He updates the website obsessively."

"What's there to update, though? Oh shit! Have you acquired some actual art? I want to see!"

"God no! We're talking margins. Fonts. It's beautiful, actually. The website. The gallery looks exactly the same."

"You know, I tell practically everyone I meet that my best friend gets paid to sit in an empty room. People think it's so awesome and creepy."

No, I hadn't wanted this. I had wanted to tell E the truth. And I had wanted her to tell it back. I had wanted her to say, "You're right, Tulip. You're pathetic."

I was a girl who did not wander, a girl who had no reason, but I had wanted her to say, "Just leave."

Leave him, Betty.

Leave and come here, to me.

27.

Hours passed. Days. Nights. I went to work, I went to work, I went to work, and what do you know? At last I had something to show for it.

I knew, for example, which blogspot would yield the recipe for the salad Sarah Smalls had picked at before a soap-opera audition one summer, which would furnish a critique of the extravagant ballroom proportions and surprising mélange of moire, silk faille, and leather in her dress the summer after that. I knew which url might offer an analysis of State Assembly Caucus Secretary Jennifer Oeuf's comments at the latest meeting of the Committee on Natural Resources and Sporting Heritage, I knew which would analyze the stats relevant to her race for state senate some months hence. I knew which bandwidth would yield the clearest picture of Calliope Pandey's mouth against her giant microphone; I knew the volume at which her voice would transmute from tin to brass.

No one could escape. My mother was mercifully hard to find at first, given her name's ambiguation, but then I remembered to add *genius* to the search box. My father popped up when I opted for *legal liability*. My brother had quit the U—school isn't everything, Betty!—but he'd kept at his lessons—the piano, the string bass, the saxophone, even that unbearable snare. My parents could never tell me where he was anymore—"He just wanders," my mother said, "I think he's depressed?"—but my screen said the Aegean (jazz cruise), said he would be ensconced next month with a sick quartet in the slick lounge of a Kyoto hotel.

And, of course, my screen told me all about E. Yes, my gossipmate had begun to pop up on gossip sites, the art-world variety, anyway. Everything was awful, or fine, actually, she guessed she was pretty good at it, so there she was—standing, contemplative, before a spattered canvas, a cup of gallery swill tilting in one hand. Or leaning forward, laughing, hand perched on the velvet lapel of an artist better known for his marriage to a fabulously wealthy and potentially demented collector forty years his senior than for his art. E was wearing a plain black shift with white fur trim; she was wearing a plain white t-shirt, a high-waisted black pencil skirt, strand after strand of black pearls; she was wearing a lacy camisole, a diaphanous caftan, and an expression of amused nonchalance.

I was not wearing anything. I was only a name. No, no one nowadays was anonymous, but I, at least, came close. The website was beautiful, actually—austere—a blank white wall behind minute black print. A dismissive description of the gallery's long history was punctuated by an ellipsis of images, photos of the wall behind me, to my left, to my right, side by side by side. Their emptiness seemed intentional in this context, but what of mine? For there I resided, six inches below; you could see me if you scrolled down. *Questions?* the website questioned. *Contact Betty Bird, 401-235-363.*

When I got married, Solly—still off at the ashram if ever online—added my revised surname to the site. He did not, however, add the missing digit.

So imagine my alarm when the slim telephone finally rang. It was a drippy dour morning in my future's gazillionth month. No, I hadn't always shown up at my receptionist's desk in the past four, or eight, or twelve. But I was there now.

"Betty?"

"Solly? Wow! Where are you?"

"Where are *you*?"

"At the gallery? I mean, you called here..."

"Right! I just didn't totally think—? I mean you're, like, married now, right? Congratulations, by the way!"

"Thanks!"

"I mean it's *so* sweet that you *are* there, it's just—how's your *mom*, by the way—oh great!—well, *any*way—the thing is—"

The thing was: he'd met this reality TV showrunner at a ~~LAN~~ lithographer's party in Antwerp (but what of the ashram?), and they'd got to talking, they'd gone out for Steenbrugge Blonds and Trappist cheeses, and Solly had directed TV Guy to our website, thinking he might have found, like, a patron? Indeed, he had! Just not the variety of patron he'd anticipated. TV Guy loved the *site's* austere aesthetic, and asked Solly to update his side project's web presence.

"He hates Hollywood," Solly said with sickening earnestness, "so he spends as much time as he can in Kauai, making midcenturyesque furniture out of repurposed surfboards! His stuff is pretty amazing actually, and he just wants people to see it, right? He really appreciates that I'm in the art world..."

So, *any*way, TV Guy had set Solly up on the island, and Solly had been, oh my god, *so* happy. Walking on the sand, pan-searing the most amazing mahi... His therapist had been right: exercise helped! And eating fresh and local... *Any*way, he started out doing odd jobs for TV Guy, some site design, some coding, and then, what do you know? He had a ton of other clients! He was designing an "existential war game" called *Dour Surfer*, and the thing was—he cleared his throat, audibly moved—he'd finally found it. He'd found his future!

"I'm not selling the gallery," he hastened to add. "It was my *father's*, you know? But, as much as I want to, I just don't have time to direct it. I've finally admitted it. It feels great!"

Was this it, then? The moment *I* would do something, because I'd been provided so many things my grandmother had or hadn't? A-one, and a-two, and a-one, two, three, four—

28.

Sorry, Lizzie.

The truth is: I had somewhere to be.

The truth is: a blue lady was silently singing, and a table awaited me.

The truth is: I was busy losing myself, with you, at the Lonesome, and maybe that's why I first suggested, and, at last, approved, E. I told her to contact Solly, not that I thought she would—it was a mean whim, a jokey challenge. I'd been calling her long-bluffed bluff ("I hate this city so fucking much"), but then I blinked and it was E's first day on the job. I blinked and my commander in chief was my commander in chief.

131

29.

Have I mentioned that E's first day was a Tuesday? That I spent said Tuesday doing the things one does in X—the coffee, the toast, the brushing of coffee and toast from teeth? That I drove to work without incident? That I perched on Solly's white chair behind Solly's white desk, while, across the room, E oversaw construction of her own?

As it turns out, years can pass when you're an art object by day, a wife turned shy barfly by night. Pretty soon you're twenty-ugh, and after that you're twenty-*ugh*. And then the Tuesday in question is the Tuesday in question.

Cut, therefore, to the June Tuesday on which I'm still sorry to have started my story, just a few minutes short of high noon:

Three teenagers assemble a ginormous, if slender, white computer, a worktable lacquered to match. E looks from them to me, from them to me again, eyes affecting wide, derisive surprise.

"This is so weird!" she calls out. "I mean, I have to say, I don't totally get it yet."

But what's not to get? The job is a good one, E's move to X a "career move," in its way. On average it takes three to five years for a gallery to make a profit, but, in this case, there will be no setup costs, no location or build-out costs. Money is no object. Solly will pay for those things he hasn't already, and E can stop researching; E can concentrate on inventory. At the tender age of twenty-*ugh*, E can restore a once-respected gallery to competence if not prominence, and I have no doubt she will.

"Oh totally..." I answer. "It's *totally* weird." We laugh. Ha ha ha ha ha ha ha ha!

"How can I help?" I hear myself call.

"How can *I*?" E throws her hands up.

But she can, she does. As I return my attention to my workstation, if not to any work, as I seek the search box only to blink blankly at the cursor, as I try not to let on that I am also looking, whenever possible, at E, she seems to forget me, forget herself. It's as if the initial pretense was enough, as if her refusal to admit her ambition and expertise outright was the very means by which she achieved them. She circles the pseudodesk, walks parallel to a wall. She stares into the plaster, retrieves a measuring tape from her purse, and counts an expanse of white nothing. Her phone rings, and she answers in a voice so brusque, so alarmingly competent, it has me clenching my fists. She makes a call, then makes some laughing suggestion to the teen tasked with the desk.

Still—when the teen who's been constructing the spinny chair asks her to take it for one—when the techie-teen wants to know whether the operating system is operating to her liking—E forgets to forget, remembers to play it both ways, to shrug over at me hammily, frown like a clown.

Is he talking to little old me? But how should I know?

I shrug back.

I don't know, E, how should you?

HOW COULD YOU!?

Better to avoid eye contact, to monitor Solly's monitor. And, hey, what do you know? Calliope Pandey is today's featured "doer" on howdoesshedoit.com! Soon E will have to admit that in winning one contest, she's lost the one that matters—the one we made all by ourselves—but for now her old buddy Calliope is corresponding from an undisclosed SUV, taking precious time from more perilous reporting to admit that she wouldn't be able to do any reporting *comfortably* if she hadn't splurged on the handmade clogs available at the link. The memory foam insoles drive the price up, but for someone who travels as much as she does? They pay for themselves! And in another window, who else smiles but Sarah Smalls? Click the little triangle and see her smear her nose with cream cheese as she lifts a bagel to laughing lips—she's just like us! Even though the dress below befits a tacky angel, a deranged and hopeful bride, what with its frothy expanses of cream tulle, its silver paillettes and feathered epaulets, its bodice of—wait! Is the whole get-up just a dressed-up version of my breakup dress?

I have half a mind to solicit E's expert opinion.

And what would she do then? Discipline me for drifting about the internet on gallery time? Sniff last night at the Lonesome on my lonesome, daytime breath? Just get it over with already and fire my ass—

Please?

Oh, please fire me, E! What better climax could we find for our epic, yearslong game of Who Cares Less?

No, if I dared invite my old gossipmate to gossip I know E would offer up more false cheer, play along, play it both ways.

That dress was too sweet for you, anyway, Tulip. You need contrast! Tension!

YOU DON'T THINK I'M TENSE ENOUGH?

My shoulders snarl. And somehow E is there without my asking, one hand on my chairback, the other resting, for some reason, on the slim white phone that never—

"Does this thing ever ring?" My eyes walk up her arm (three-quarter-length sleeves, faint gray plaid), they step upon her smiling face. "I don't get it. Where did Solly sit when you were both here?"

"We weren't."

"How is that possible?"

"I mean maybe for a few hours during my first month or something? It's hard to remember. But I guess I'd just, like—" o sing of a girl who does not "—wander?"

E whistles. "Talk about a manager! If that's not its own species of genius I don't know what is."

"But you're a genius, too," I say. "And, hey, who are *we* to presumptuously dispense with the Snodgrass legacy? Tell those nine-year-olds to go home already." I stand up. "Take the desk. Come on, take it! I can wander."

At last, something seems to flicker in E, a chill gusting across her gaze when she catches sight of tall Sarah Smalls made small by Solly's screen. She takes a deep breath, puts both hands on the chairback, as if bracing for some terrible truth. *I want this, don't I?*

"Speaking of the nine-year-olds," E whispers, "I'm pretty sure they're going to be a while? I'm also pretty sure they've figured out I have no clue what I'm doing and can't answer any of their questions. So, what do you say we blow off work for a bit? Go to lunch?"

You tell me, Mr. President! Tell me what to wear! Where to go!

She blinks.

I mean, you're the boss, right? And I am but your Girl Friday!?

"Girl Friday?"

Wait... Am I saying these lines out loud?

E laughs. "So you're a Carib cannibal now? I thought appropriating Edo courtesans was more your speed."

Carib cannibal?

"You know, *Robinson Crusoe*? Should I teach you English and convert you to Christianity? Save your father from ambush? Oh, come on, Tulip. You took Literatures of Empire with me. Professor Kraft? Pleated cords, creepy leer? Come, my little cannibal, let me feed you. Come *on*, Tulip. This is *too* weird. Let's get out of here. Let's go to lunch!"

30.

Have you ever seen *Mid-Wilshire*, Lizzie?

If you've already written a paper on, say, the aesthetics of immaterial labor in early-century MTV programming, please forgive the following exegesis.

Mid-Wilshire is named for the LA neighborhood to which its stars—Becky, the hard-eyed and headbanded twenty-something protagonist, and Kimsy, her accomplice and antagonist-to-be—move in the first episode. In theory, the series centers on Becky's personal and professional "dramz," as the promotional materials call them, as she endeavors not just to "come of age" but also to "have it all."

But, in practice, each episode consists of a dramzy voiceover ("I was so excited about my new job at *Cute-tourier Magazine*, but then my best friend, Kimsy, had to show up drunk to my boss's knitwear show!!!") prefacing an utterly dramz-less sequence of illegible stares, bitten bottom lips, nigh-on imperceptible nods, panicked glances off camera, and explosively avoid-tational lines like, "No, it's fine, we're totally fine, it was just, you know, like, a work thing? But it's fine now? I mean [long pause] I honestly don't even know what to say about it?"

Oh the dramz!

Dramz to set Guy Greco to on-the-record sneering ("I mean, it's Whole Foods. It's a couple of sorority girls shopping at Whole Foods. Not knowing whether your hair is blond or brown is not a narrative conflict"). Dramz, in other words, for which E and I were impeccably trained.

In its third season, *Mid-Wilshire* reached what might be considered a climax, airing its most memed scene. Kimsy is rumored to have spread a rumor/comment on capitalism that Becky was so dismayed by the dust on her dressing table that she threatened to call ICE on her housekeeper, but neither star's contract will allow her to acknowledge, onscreen, a conflict that arose off it. During yet another night out at Club Cloud, Kimsy's evil boyfriend, Sven, advises her to roll up on Becky and politely inquire as to why she is being so cold. Upon said rolling, Becky does some rolling of her own (her eyes are wide and blue, liberally mascaraed), before fleeing from banquette to bathroom, from bathroom to bar, from bar to back exit. Kimsy follows, biting her now surgically enhanced bottom lip.

And then—the face-off! Though the faces in question remain averted from one another throughout...

> KIMSY
> (*quietly, looking down*)

Will you just? I mean...could you maybe answer me? I mean, whatever, it's *fine*, but, like...what did I...do?

> BECKY
> (*eyes averted, hand raised, whispering*)

You...know what you "did," Kimsy.

> KIMSY
> (*to the floor*)

Okay, yeah. I mean, it's fine, it's totally fine, but, like, I'm not sure I...totally...understand?

> BECKY
> (*to the door, barely audible*)

You know [extremely long pause] what you "did"...

Wasn't this also true of E? Didn't she recognize that though I got her the job, I never ever meant for her to take it? Anyway, now that she'd come back to me only to loom just beyond my reach, didn't she at least know the price—didn't she know enough to let me win my rightful prize?

I was the best at caring the least!

I'd been the best all along!

But I wasn't the one who had to say it.

Which is, itself, to say: wasn't it about time for our climax? (I wanted this, didn't I?) Anyway, I can see it now:

INT. RESTAURANT – TUESDAY IN QUESTION

BETTY
(*voiceover*)

So what if the one thing that had changed at the gallery in ~~several~~ ~~some~~ not so many years was my boss? By the Tuesday in question, it was E. Yes, *E*. My old gossipmate. My old getting-it-mate. My roommate at the distinguished institution I shall hereupon refer to as "the U." But so what?

E

Oh my god, this looks so good! What are you going to get!? I, like, can't choose. Ugh! You pick, and I'll just order whatever you order, Tulip.

TULIP
(*whispering*)

Really? Is that really how you're going to play this?

E

Um? [Long pause] Um?

Yes, I can see it now, that quiet apocalypse of apologies and almost-accusations. And I can hear myself whispering, a la Becky, at long last, "I am so fucking mad right now."

But how could I make like Becky on the Tuesday in question, when E wasn't making like Kimsy, when E wasn't confessing her insincere incomprehension, but was, instead, getting me yet again?

"I mean, look, you know I get it. Obviously we both get that this whole situation is super weird, but, like—"

But, like—how had this happened!?

One minute we were staring at our menus, the next E was slamming the gas, smash-crashing forward, free, for some reason, to follow an unprecedented and utterly uncoy script:

"It's super *super* weird, but here's the thing—" She looked at me, eyes wide, liberally mascaraed. "I *know* you, Tulip. And I know you get it."

I looked down—think about the table, Betty!—but could feel E's unashamed eyes on me.

"What I'm saying is, I know—we both know—this—" I looked up in time to see her cordon off the words with quoting fingertips: "—'career thing' has always been—" She rolled her eyes, pushing the next word away: "—*fraught* for you—"

Then she dropped her apologetic hands. Her gaze flew at me. "Betty, the situation's weird. But what matters is I can finally help!"

[Long pause]

"Will you listen to me for once in your lucky, fucking life? I really want to help you."

[Long pause]

"I've always wanted to."

[Long pause]

"Don't you see? I'm *actually* in a position to help you!"

She refused to fill the next [long pause].

"You want to help me," I finally managed, "with my... 'career'?"

E nodded, plainly. She'd come back to me, she was right there, and yet I'd never seen her like this, so bare. Her eyes were warm pools, her expression generous and unprotected and terribly, terribly cruel. I can almost swear I did what I did next for her.

I laughed: Ha!

Ha ha ha ha ha ha ha ha ha.

"You think I *care* about my" ha ha "career?"

E sighed. "What's going on this time? Whatever it is, you can tell me. I mean you know I'll—wait, are you crying?"

Ha ha? "You really don't get it? You really don't know I have bigger problems?"

"Are you talking about—?"

"No, you're right, you're right. They're not *that* bad. 'Problems'—ha!" Conflicts! Climaxes! "That *is* a little much. I shouldn't be so self-aggrandizing! They're just…incidents… Nothing more!"

"Betty, I wish you would just—"

"The truth is—" I said. "The truth is—"

But it would have been too kind to tell E the truth.

So I did what I had to do. I took the necessary action. I made the frames flicker. I made my dear best friend disappear.

31.

I raised a hand, and, poof, she wasn't there. Blink, blink: bye-bye, E, hello, waitress, who was nodding and smiling and saying, Yes, *to*tally—getting me in a way E never could. Oh *yes*, the waitress agreed, there was nothing *like* a good Chablis—of course there were so many awful bottles that people forgot how sublime a really *minerally* Chablis could be—but she had just the vintage for me, her dearest bestest friend, Betty B.

And blink, drink, the waitress was right, the wine was perfect, because E was fading, drink, blink, E was the cumulous-headed lady at the next table, turning as I lurched, gasping as I lifted my napkin from the floor, as I crumpled it into a rose and flung. Brava! Encore! Or no—Cloudlady was merely saying, "What the—?" as I lifted bottle from table, took one last minerally sip, then turned from Betty into Becky, turned all the way away from my own personal Kimsy (oh the dramz!), turned and stormed from the scene.

Blink: no more E!

Blink, blink: goodbye, goodbye!

She was the gaspless girl at the grocery store now, the one snapping her gray gum and scanning my Grand Marnier with stunning nonchalance, not minding my hiccuping and swaying, not even caring to check my ID.

Of course the Grand Marnier was for the man I've claimed I will not name's duck à l'orange, but why not pour a touch or two into my personal tumbler, because fuck it if this recipe didn't take forever? So blink, drink, and E had disappeared, all my incidents unheard, vanished, poof, just like her. Drink, drink, drink, and E was—ha ha!—Orson. She was slinking through her doggy door and pawing the lower cupboards, trying to reach her long tongue above the counter, where my half-full tumbler sat. Oh, sure, little buddy, why not? Why not have a lick, have a drink, so that you-he-she might turn into me—smiling into the steamy oven window, into my puddled plate, into the high sheen of that teak table, then into the rearview at last, as College Street turned to Scholar Street turned to Gown, which would take me all the way down.

Had dinner happened, then? Was the duck à l'orange already in the trash, H's *I was thinking we should bring a baby into this* in the paaaaaaghst? Quite right! After all, this was not a song of husbands. I wasn't going to make it about him, no matter what questions E asked.

Poof!

She was a blue woman in the sky now, she was neon, blinking on, blinking off.

Blink, drink, blink, and E was Goodman, saying, "So what if you don't want a dog? Don't you want a baby?" and Sunshine saying, "I lost you there, Betty!"

Drink, drink, and she was my silver grandmother, ~~Ingrid Bergman,~~ she was my mother, tsk-tsking, saying she'd trained me for this but also for something other, saying, "Betty, oh how did you get *here*?"

"I've got you," she was saying.

"I'll get you…"

And she was you, Lizzie Barmaid. A face, a circle, blinking. Mere feet away, too close, too far. I was reaching, I needed to be steadied. I put my hand on the table lip, pushed or smashed. Or were those my empties crashing to the floor? "Um…Goodman?" My other hand was clasping at his sleeve, grasping for something steady as I stood. "Goodman?" But he was you, Lizzie. Smashing, crashing, strobing closer, crying "Betty!" Yes, you were saying my name, I was almost sure, and I was saying something else, something about *incidents* and *have I mentioned* and *actually the truth is*, or no, no, I couldn't say that to your face, so I was spewing something other, something about a mother or a baby, *oh baby I want this I motherfucking want this*, something about a lost best friend, but no, because I didn't come here for your face like a spotlight, didn't come here to speak or spew, certainly didn't come here for—

"Betty!" you cried, and you were closer, reaching. Something was coming out of my mouth, something other.

2 tbsp butter

3 tsp Grand Marnier

¼ tsp orange bitters

Something orange was coming out of my mouth. "Betty!" you cried because I was doing it, I was spewing my husband's favorite all over the table. A sprig of rosemary. (Had I forgotten to chew?) An orange segment, or its remnant. Zest! Goodman and Sunshine were screeching their chairs back, but you were close, Lizzie, you were leaning in, and, relieved, at last, I was reaching. My arm like a beam, *I sing of arms and the man*, reaching for a face that was the necessary spotlight. The face that was an inch from my eyes, shaping the word *Betty*. "Are you okay?—it's okay, I've got you, I'll get you—" The face that was spotlight, searchlight, dashing flashlight, moving through the Lonesome's dim glimmer until it stopped in the bathroom's bombed-out crater, rough paper towels crawling around my wet mouth. The face that was next to my face, then, in the scrawled-over back-hall mirror. The face that was asking how I got here, and promising you already knew.

Cindy Sherman
Untitled Film Still #12, 1978
Gelatin silver print, 20.3 x 25.4 cm / 8 x 10 in

ℬ
CRASH!

I.

Lizzie Barmaid and I had been here before, not so many months prior to the Tuesday in question. In the Lonesome Ballroom's back hallway, facing one another in the mirror, talking about who else but Guy Greco.

"I mean, just imagine if, like, *I* did that!" she'd said. "Or, oh my god, *you*, what if *you* were a filmmaker and you did that?"

"Did what?"

"*You* know! Performed your insanely normative hyperfemininity. It wouldn't work. Like, you couldn't wear *that* dress and talk about how you got a Peaches 'n Cream Barbie for your fifth birthday and how you write your screenplays at your dressing table or whatever."

"I guess it's a good thing I'm not a filmmaker!"

"'Where does the violence come from, Mr. Greco?' I mean, has anyone ever asked you where the *passivity* comes from?"

Lizzie picked at something on her forehead, ran her finger over a single magnificent brow. I waited, but her show had stopped as suddenly as it began. How I wished it would start up again—

O Muse, tell me the causes!
"Yeah," I tried, "totally..." But my voice sounded swallowed; the jukebox was loud. Goodman was playing Sinatra again—"A Very Good Year." "It's like this song, right? Imagine if one of us—"

But I didn't have to imagine. Just like that, Lizzie Barmaid was singing:

When I was seventeen, it was a very good year!
It was a very good year for telling my boyfriend I loved giving head
'Cause I thought it made me sound cool!
We'd meet behind the school...
He'd leave me to clean the cum out of my hair...
It was a very good year...

And then it was my turn to sing, Lizzie's turn to swing her surprised face:

When I was ni-i-neteen, it was a very good year!
It was a very good year to give this guy a bunch of handjobs
To help with his 'medical condition'!
Once my wrist was in position...
His jizz poured sweet and clear...
It was a very good year...

And as I stumbled from the mirror to Goodman's table, Lizzie's dizzy laughter in my ear, Goodman seemed to see something in my face. He smiled, stood, started to serenade: his days were blah-blah, he was in the autumn of his blah-blah... I'd come here to listen to him, but I wasn't now, not really. And when he cried, "Come on, Betty, sing with me!" I was no more able to join in his song than he'd been able to join in ours. It was all I could do to tame my smile. Was Lizzie Barmaid finally my friend? Had we just become confidants? Conspirators? What, I kept thinking, would happen now?

2.

At first, there were a couple of happenings. A collision by the jukebox the next night, so late that every denizen of the LB (except LB, I presume) was wildly drunk. I'd been waiting to put a song on, and I hadn't been aware that the woman in front of me was her—because wasn't our barmaid behind the bar still, didn't I hear her shake-shake-shaking? But no, the finger with the long black nail punching B2 as if to push off from it was Lizzie's, and the body that whirled in response, bumping softly into mine, was Lizzie's, too.

"It's you!" she said—a beautiful phrase, the one I'd had in mind myself.

But then she said, "Can you fucking believe her? Like, I'm sorry, but wearing a playsuit with glittery hearts on it is not a 'seditious response to the male gaze.' Not when your ass is hanging out."

Three grad-student dudes (aquarium glasses, conscientiously disarranged hair) were sitting at a table behind Goodman's, their eyes swimming toward the girl who sat—all by herself—across from them. Her hands were folded on the tabletop, her posture authoritative yet somehow deferential. She might have been at a job interview, had it not been for the playsuit. Its scattered hearts seemed to beat. I couldn't make out the girl's face.

"Do you think she's pretty?" Lizzie asked.

But wouldn't it be embarrassing to admit I was conversant in her rhetoric? Then again, it's not like I didn't know the answer, whether I could get a good look at the girl in question or not.

And later—that night or that week, I'm not sure—a voice filled the room and our eyes met. What do you know? Sinatra was seventeen again! Our eyes met, they rolled, our smiles moved at the same speed, because Sinatra was always seventeen.

But did Lizzie know I was the one to push F3? Yes, this time I'd done it—to please Goodman or Lizzie Barmaid, I wasn't sure.

Or maybe I'd put the song on for myself. However objectionable, it is also one of my all-time favorites.

3.

What would happen now!?

What traction had I gained with my maybe-confidant, what action would my new union with Lizzie incite? Would we spike Goodman's drinks or water them down; would we sic Sunshine on the (un)pretty girl in the glitter hearts?

Would we at least meet at the mirror again?

Maybe Lizzie was embarrassed. She'd revealed her vulnerability in the face of a playsuit, her fluency in a grandmother's rhetoric. Then again, maybe the explanation was simpler. Every time I saw Lizzie Barmaid after that, I was sitting at Goodman's table, and the rule had not changed.

She lifted my glass. I looked away. "Charles, James." For a long time, I didn't say anything.

But, though I spoke less than ever, I felt ever more spoken to: *Did Violet Flowers really—? Are these assholes actually—? Don't you have anything better—anything other—?*

Her eyes questioned me that week and the next week. They questioned me in February, May. They questioned me on Sunday and on Monday. And they questioned me on the Tuesday in question, chiming in time with the Lonesome lady's light, Lizzie thlunking angry empties onto her tray. They flashed—*how did you even*—as her mouth asked, "Betty? Are you okay?" As she strobed closer, caught my arms in hers. As she helped me from the table, helped me to the bathroom. As she picked half-digested duck from my hair. As she wiped my mouth. And now, in the mirror, at last Lizzie's mouth and eyes matched. She looked at me. And asked the big question aloud.

"How did you get here?"

You. Not your mother. Not your grandmother.

Lizzie Barmaid and I were the same age. It had been argued that ours (like our mothers' and grandmothers' before us!) was the first generation of women whose futures were entirely open, whose fates could take any imaginable shape. So why did mine—"How did you get here?" Lizzie repeated—look like *this*?

I looked at her: the glinting nose, the careful brows, the ensemble that had been assembled to express both rejection and invitation, to say fuck the patriarchy but while you're at it fuck me, oh yes, just like that, no harder, ha-fucking-arder. Lizzie Barmaid's delicate care was gorgeous, it was wretched. I looked at her looking at me, teetering on her tough heels, tired from so many days spent staring at Chantal Akerman's kitchens or Cindy Sherman's stuck shifting face, from so many nights scuffing from bar to table to table to bar, getting paid too little to ferry drinks to Goodman and other good men. I looked at her, and I understood: Lizzie Barmaid wanted my answer because she needed a story of her own.

And I swear I was about to tell the whole truth, the old ugly truth, when LB sighed and said, "I'm going to need your keys if you have them. Did you drive? Come on, Betty, will you please just tell me how you got here?"

Lizzie Barmaid needn't have worried.

I said it: "I never drive."

4.

But what else was that crash, or, at very least, that controlled car-door detonation? Why was my foot feeling for the brake, my fist finding its way to Reverse? Why was Gown turning to Scholar to College, tall houses blinking blue hellos, black treetops flapping past like merry crows?

Why were the numbers of the digital speedometer flipping like the windy pages of a calendar in the kind of movie I used to watch with my grandmother?

Why was the windshield whirling?

And why was a house twirling up, hurling itself toward the glass?

5.

Matt Eats a Sandwich came out nearly twenty years after the Tuesday in question, and when it did Guy Greco was everywhere. Critics hailed *Matt* as Greck's first masterwork since *B/S*. There was no need then to turn Guy Greco to the object of a morning web-stalk, to type his name into that ceaselessly blinking box. There he was, Ex-Boyfriend G, floating beside a telephonic rain cloud; there he was, glaring from the side of a bus, arm still struggling to encircle the massive shoulders of Jake Rock. There he was, making like my mother in another *Sunday Magazine*, collapsed on a collapsible chaise longue that was de-collapsed upon a gleaming golf green. He wore his signature flannel and mud-streaked jeans, work boots crossed delicately at the ankle. Mountains loomed. High palms seemed to sway. Even at that scale, amid those towering rocks and trees, G's sideburns went on and on.

So did the reporter. He spent several hundred words on the interview's setting, a private golf course in the shadow of Mount San Jacinto whose ball-washers had been designed by Eero Saarinen ("a collision of the elemental and the manmade that might have been manufactured by Greco's own mad mind"); nearly a hundred more attempting to render the tone of G's baritone drone. Could you blame the guy for expending a half page describing the "indescribable" *Matt Eats a Sandwich* ("an unflinching epic of ideas that takes on the nature of modern warfare, the cost of industrial decline, the relationship between corporations and desire, not to mention pornography, flânerie, the relative merits of Wendy's Crispy Chicken Sandwich, Los Angeles in the collective imagination, prostate cancer, climate change, and golf")? And a seeming tangent about our reporter's lactose intolerance segued with surprising ease into an anecdote about the besotted teenagers sitting beside him at an early screening: as the lights went down, the boy was hand-feeding his date Milk Duds; as they came up, he was doubled over, weeping, pushing the uncomprehending girl away.

I expected the interview to end as they all do: with our reporter venting about his subject's astounding talent for circumvention. Because good old Greck was now famed for exchanges such as the following:

REPORTER: Can you talk a little bit about your relationship with Jake R—?

G: Can you believe they call this the desert? Of course, the Cahuilla called it Se-Khi—you know what that means, right?

REPORTER: I—

G: Boiling water. But I'm cold, man.

REPORTER: I've actually been thinking how hot you must be in all that flannel. I mean it's—

G: (*whispering*) *Se. Fucking. Khi.* They've fucked it all up, though, right? Patton should have blown it up when he had the chance. Blown himself up too...

So imagine my surprise when the reporter asked a question seven pages in that caught Ex-Boyfriend G's fancy, and had him expending several hundred words of his own.

"I heard a rumor," the reporter huffed—G was sprinting past hole sixteen in an effort to "warm up," our reporter struggling to keep up—"that you cut a lengthy flashback from the scene at the abandoned woodshed in Brentwood—"

Guy Greco stopped midstride. "Let me ask *you* something. Why do you think they're called *flash*backs? Why do you think I make *flicks*?"

According to Guy, any flashback, let alone a lengthy one, was a sure sign of a static story. Make that no story.

It was at that point that good old Guy began to make like his sideburns, going on and on, supporting his thesis with citations, just as he'd been taught at the U.

Picture it, he instructed our reporter: our heroine is standing on a veranda, blinking into the windows blinking up from below... She brushes a tear from her eye, she leans into the distant light...

Is she going to jump!?

If only! Just as the viewer's heart starts to trip in anticipation, he hears the telltale harp, and the heroine's face goes hazy. She's remembering her childhood bedroom, her father yelling because she left her blanket on the heater and blah blah blah... So I ask you, GG asked the reporter, why the veranda? And wherefore the yacht's proud prow, whereupon another ingénue thinks of a grandparent, lost on the Lusitania? Why decorate the drawing room if our heroine is only going to stand there and stare through the window, if she is only going to gaze, prehaze, into the fireplace, or into the painting hanging above it—a painting in which yet another still heroine stands! Why do we, the audience, need to stare into her stare? Just because some starlet's hands grip a steering wheel, doesn't mean she's going anywhere. And we get it already! She is overborne by memories of her overbearing mother! So just give us the mother, the father, the grandfather before him. Start at the start.

I stopped reading. Contemplated my navel, my teacup, wished that the steam wisping from it would fade into the hypercritical, if hypocritical, face of Lizzie Barmaid. "Doesn't he have, like, handlers?" she'd say, delighted. "Isn't there someone he pays to point out that every scene he insults stars a woman?"

But, like I said, nearly twenty years had passed. I hadn't seen Lizzie Barmaid since the night in question.

6.

I hadn't seen Lizzie since I told her I walked to the bar, and she walked out of its back hallway. I could wait here, she said, collect myself. But she was going to get me a ride, call me a cab, something. She'd drive me herself if it came to that, but, don't worry, she was going to get me home.

"Sorry," I said.

Lizzie looked at me oddly. *Don't be such a fucking—* "Betty, don't worry about those assholes. They're not even going to remember that. Seriously, if I had a dime for every time someone's thrown up in here!" She put a hand on my shoulder. "I've got you," she said. "I'm going to go get that cleaned up, and just trust me, it'll be like nothing happened."

"Nothing?"

Nothing nothing nothing nothing nothing—

She held me by both shoulders now. "I swear. Leave it to me, Betty, and it will be like you were never here."

7.

In that case, might as well cut to a clip from *Matt Eats a Sandwich*! High noon. A screen caught inside our screen: a mud-spattered driver's-side window. Jake Rock is Matt Stone this time, and Matt

Stone is a trapped blur in the glass, a blur that traps another blur within. A vehicle has pulled up alongside his. He rolls down his window. The other window lowers in turn. There is a man at the wheel, an old man. Hair like a shredded shark's fin, strangely sharp teeth. The man's grin glints. His engine revs. "Dad," Rock/Stone whispers. "You bastard!"

And then—? The car chase to end all car chases! Those are Guy's words, anyway.

REPORTER: Is perfection a burden for you? Like, how do you top the climax of this one?

G: (*voice catching*) I don't. It's the climax to end all climaxes. The car chase to end all car chases.

Except it's not a car chase, exactly: it's a beat-up pickup chase; Rock/Stone and Dad-You-Bastard drive the very same unassuming make. And they are not grinding their gears along a winding mountainside, or burning across a burned-up desert, or blasting open an empty highway. No, Rock/Stone and Dad-You-Bastard are somehow going 75, 95, 105 through a tree-choked forest, a forest that is alive with dying birds' cries. They swerve around ancient redwoods, around fawns with sweetly speckled rumps, they crush the mushroomy underbrush, they crash through hectare after coniferous hectare, until, at last, their trucks fly up and through the tree canopy, in a single beautiful arc.

Inside Rock/Stone's cab, the world turns green, as pine needles whirl around the windshield. Our hero can no longer see Dad-You-Bastard and Dad-You-Bastard can no longer see him. Finally, Rock/Stone can squeeze his eyes shut, squeeze out a single tear as he submits to memory, he's just turned five, and Dad-You-Bastard has said this is Fluffmouth's day to die, and so little Rock/Stone (Pebble?) is lifting the rifle, steady, steady—

8.

On the Tuesday in question—or was it Wednesday—surely midnight had come and gone already—my foot didn't even seem to touch the gas. But the numbers on the digital speedometer were flipping like windy pages. And a familiar house was flying at my windshield.

I should get to the crash then, correct?

Headlights pushing the bushes apart, flowers like cosmic flares?

But here's the thing. I still haven't told the whole truth. I still haven't finished my song.

So?

Sorry, Guy, but you said yourself that climaxes are over. Why not cue the haze? Why not make like you and cue the motherfucking harp?

9.

Have I mentioned Henry?

My husband?

I have?

Have I mentioned Henry's ~~incidents infidelitycidents~~ infidelity?

I *haven't*?

I *forgot*?

Well, that's funny...

No, really, it's funny! Really: ha ha ha ha ha!

Ha ha ha! Ha ha ha! Ha ha ha! Ha—oh my god, stop—ha ha—it's too much!—ha ha ha—I'm crying now—ha—I'm laughing so ha ha hard I'm—ha ha ha—crying—ha ha ha ha ha hate

The truth was, I hated Henry. The truth was, I'd loved him once, I'd loved him.

10.

Disappointed?
　Think how I felt!

11.

Sorry, Guy, but I'm going to have to cut to the meet-cute.
　I was standing on my parents' front porch, trying to light a cigarette. Henry was standing on his, a hand shading his eyes, so that he might better stare contemplatively into the distance. His abstracted gaze was as intentionally professorial as his dress. He sighed, deliberately, as if to indicate the great weight of his intellect.
　I laughed—ha ha ha ha ha ha ha ha ha!
　Henry turned, arranged his features into an expression of friendliness, called out, "Hi there," his arm a maniacal windshield wiper.
　I rolled my eyes. *Hi there.* I moved my hand from side to unhappy side. Then Henry walked to the edge of his porch, and I walked to the edge of mine, said my name.
　"Betty, how old fashioned! No, no, I mean, it's charming." Then he nodded toward the cigarette I was fiddling with, rearranged his features to reveal pained sympathy. "Trying to quit?"
　Ha ha ha ha ha! "Trying to start."
　The truth was, I saw the casting breakdown as soon as I saw Henry. I knew the obvious plots this professor got caught in, knew there was no way I would ever—could ever—
　Which meant I was safe. Which meant I could do—or at least say—anything I pleased in his presence.
　For example: "I don't really smoke. I guess I'm just trying to look cool?" Smoking was bad for me, I knew, but here's the thing: I was already bad. I was a loser who lived with her parents, who

went to work in the morning but did no work all day, who was paid—during this fucked-up time in the world, no less!—to sit quiet in a chair.

Henry looked at me with eyes so intent they might have been fashioned from silver acetate. But he didn't say the words I'd heard all my life. "I'm sure you're very accomplished. Hey! Don't laugh." Though he was laughing with seeming joy as he added, "You seem smart! And I haven't talked to anyone really smart in ages."

"Aren't you a professor?"

Henry beamed. "Yes!" he professed.

"And you never talk to anyone smart at your job? Speaking of which, how'd you get *here*?"

"What do you mean?"

"You do realize you're standing around on your porch staring into space? It's the middle of the workday, man! My job's not really, like, a *job* job, nobody cares if I take a four-hour lunch, but don't you have anything better to do?"

Henry wrenched his face into a comical grimace—ha! No classes or office hours on Tuesdays. But I was right, he should be working. The thing was—he winched his shoulders up a notch, heaved a spectacular sigh—the writing wasn't going well. "Have you seen *The Lady from Shanghai*?"

"I always liked Rita Hayworth as a blonde."

"So you know it?"

"*Know* it?" I boomed, in my best near-baritone. "'If I'd known where it would end, I'd never have let anything start!'" Orson Welles's was the greatest speaking voice in the history of American cinema, but I could try anything with the artless Professor Henry as my audience.

"Whoa! Can you do the whole opening monologue?"

"Probably, but it's not my best material."

"What is?"

"I think I have almost all of *Gaslight* down. And *How to Marry a Millionaire* maybe?"

"You're kidding."

"I never kid."

"I actually haven't seen *Gaslight*. I mean, obviously, I know the psychotherapy term, or whatever." This wasn't actually so obvious back in that dark non-era. "But I thought the source material itself was sort of minor?"

"Sort of."

Henry ha-ed. "And *How to Marry a Millionaire*... I mean, I see the aesthetic import, given what they did with CinemaScope, but the antifeminism alone..."

I roughened and quickened my speech so that I made a passable Bacall (marriage was the grandest thing one could do in life, dah-ling), then shifted to Marilyn Monroe's candied whisper (men didn't make passes at lasses who wore, etc.), apologies to my grandmother.

"See?" Henry said. "It's terrifying!"

But my not-yet-husband did not yet appear terrified. His eyes were lead on the pedal, they were fast, close. Dive out of the way, Betty! But no, I held his gaze. I could never love him.

"What's your problem with *The Lady from Shanghai*?" I asked. "Besides *its* insane misogyny?"

Ha ha ha ha ha ha ha ha ha! Well! The thing was, Henry was working on this article... He was actually attempting to defend the studio-imposed score, those unsubtle strings Welles himself had hated. "I'm contending that the aggressive artifice of the music adds something. And I think Orson saw it too, eventually. But I'm stuck on this one paragraph. Actually! I could really use fresh eyes?" His own fresh eyes were smashing forward, crashing into mine. "Would you, I don't know, I mean, would *you* look at it?"

"Why would you want me to do that?"

"You just quoted my central text from memory. You obviously have some—" he grinned, intentionally unabashed "—expertise?"

I laughed in spite of myself. Ha ha ha ha ha ha ha ha hate hate hate hate hate! "You don't know me at all."

12.

But I had a problem.

Soon enough, my guilefully guileless neighbor knew all about the blank walls that blinked back at me in the gallery, the hours I spent imagining those inert planes as active appraisers, imagining myself as viable art. He knew I'd only ever been good until all at once I turned bad, that my lowest grade in high school was an A-/B+, oh damn you, Mr. Bower, and damn you, Algebra II. We stood apart on our respective porches, and then we stood together on his. We sat side by side in his porch swing, its chains marking the creaky minutes as we two tipped forth and back. We sat inside, in his office, I in his spinny ergonomic chair, doing my best, bluntest Greck—"Isn't this well-trod ground?"—Henry hovering, heaving, "Ugh! You're so right." But why even think of Boyfriend G now, in the warmth of Henry's faith? Why had I ever? I spun left, then right (so right!). "What does 'extraordinarily extradiagetic' mean?" I asked, and, "Who's the 'semiological *sujet*' in this sentence?" Until we adjourned to the living room, to the gondola sofa I'd begun to mark as my own with smears of Premier Rouge. "I'll walk you home," he always, preposterously, said, but we didn't stop walking when we reached my parents' porch. We circled the block, whispering, we stumbled into each other like drunks, and the truth was, I was falling in—

13.

Disappointed?

I know. And I wish I could say it wasn't so, but I'm afraid the evidence argues otherwise.

Exhibit A: I am turning twenty-ugh at midnight, I am lying in my childhood bed. Henry has told me to watch the window, he has a birthday surprise. I wait, remembering a ~~not-so~~-long-ago night when I lay like this, my eyes open though I told them to close, because the sooner I slept the sooner it would be tomorrow. I am remembering my father's blue shape in the doorway, his audible smile as he said "last night in the single digits" when I see the flash. It is October, dry and already cold, but there is lightning in my bedroom, there is a large summer lightning bug, swooping. I jump up, run to the glass. Henry turns the flashlight off, and I see his dim, dumb form. His hand flickers on, off, on. I can't see his face, but I know he is grinning. "This is stupid," I say, out loud. But, like my not-yet-husband, I am grinning; like a naïve nine-year-old on the night before her birthday, I am grinning, so hopeful, so hopeless.

Exhibit B: My father drops his fork. "What *is* that?" He stands, parts the leaves of the spider ivy on the sill. "Are you kidding," he says, sounding for a moment uncannily like E. "Is that Sinatra?" My mother leaps up from the table, joins him at the window. "It's the one he sang with his daughter, isn't it? So weird that they recorded a romantic duet!" Absolutely! Which is one of many, many reasons that I remain in my seat. That I shade then cover my eyes. No, I do not want to watch Henry's performance, do not want to see the proud, sheepish expression he's no doubt contrived for his serenading face. I should be covering my ears because, yes, I'm not kidding you, Dad, I despise the same old lies, but Henry's gone and ruined it all by saying something stupid like I love you. I love you I love you I love you, he croons, and I should be covering my mouth, because I'm doing it again, I'm smiling, ugh, smiling.

Exhibit C: It is cold, December already, almost Christmas, but Henry and I sit cross-legged on the lawn. The stiff grass will show our shapes when we stand. And then? We will be separated! For two whole weeks! We gaze at one another, not speaking. Henry's hand floats from the grass, hovers beside my cheek. His knuckles graze my skin and his fingers fill my hair, he pulls at my ponytail, his grasp tender, enraged. My hair falls loose. "You should wear it down more," he rasps. He takes my hand, twists my sparkly green hair elastic around my ring finger. Plucks a cold blade from the ground and wraps it around his own.

Exhibit D: I spend the next two weeks in Amsterdam, where my mother is receiving a prize for the fearlessness of her artistic practice. "Maybe they mean fraudulence?" she jokes. "Maybe something got lost in translation?" For years now, she points out, she's been too fear*ful* to practice much at all. She hasn't created anything truly new since *The Creation*... So she won't mind if I spend the next two weeks making like she did in the months after the opening— depressed because the best is behind me, back in X? She won't mind if I turn my hotel bed to a soft and lovelorn coffin? Not at all! But my father minds. He's at the foot, saying, "How old are you, how *spoiled* are you? It's after eleven. Get up!" I get up. I stroll lugubriously beside a canal. I eat stroopwafels and smoutballen. I stare into good old van Gogh's bad old face, which glowers beneath straw hat, felt hat, no hat. I sit in the Concertgebouw, and listen to Mozart's *Sinfonia Concertante* for violin and viola, and wish myself back to the frozen grass. I sit on the overstuffed hotel armchair and listen to my father yell through the phone at Danny, who is not far away, according to an indiscreet screen in an internet café. *Questa sera, presso La Casa del Jazz!* "There's an overnight train from Rome. You know we'll pay for it..." "He's just drifting," my mother whispers at me from her own chair, "and probably drinking too much. You know what he needs? An organized woman who's sure of what she wants, who'll whip him into shape!" "How old are you?" my father yells, but not at Danny. I am asleep again, it seems. "Get up!" All the while, the sparkly elastic winds around my fourth finger. We are in a restaurant on the Kalverstraat, I am eating a mutton pie doused in vinegar and dusted with horseradish, when my father points at the green hair tie and says, "What *is* that?"

Exhibit E: My parents have slept on the plane. My parents have slept at the gate. My parents have slept on the next plane, my father's arms a pointy pillow on his tray table, my mother's head knocking the shade. I have not slept. Not in the first plane and not in the second. I have not slept on the layover and I do not sleep in the taxi. It has snowed today, and our pseudocity is a smooth and splendid bedsheet, but still I do not sleep. When we turn onto our street, I see him. He is sitting on his porch steps, and in the distance he looks like a lonely little boy, a latchkey kid, locked out. But he sees the taxi and stands, he starts running across his white lawn. My father is fumbling in his pockets for money to pay the driver when he says, "Oh, just get out already." And I am out, I am running through the snow in my thin canvas sneakers, my socks are wet and my feet are wet and Henry, the man I would-never-could-never love, is in my arms. Our breath rises around us in clouds; I cannot tell which clouds belong to me. In the morning, I will wake and look out the window. I will see our footprints, a single, singing line in the snow.

14.

When I announced my engagement to Henry, no one objected.

Sure, years later, my mother and E would both object to this claim. They'd claim they told me so, they told me no, they begged me not to make my terrific mistake.

But I remember a dreamy bedroom calm in my mother's voice, a variety I hadn't heard since the year after her *Creation* opened to the world and she had trouble opening her blinds, opening her eyes. I would fold myself in bed beside her, ask about the future by asking about the past. *What did he look like? Where did you meet?* "It's very fast," she said now, "but, well, you must be—" hysterical? ill? "excited..." Of course, she'd trained me for something other... Transhistorical feminist aesthetics, however invisible! Gender nihilism, however implicit! But as she knew: she'd trained me for this, too.

And I remember E's collusive, corrosive humor some months later, when I mustered up my courage, if not to engage in an honest conversation, then to say the word *engaged*. "Should we double-wedding it?" she said. "I'm pretty sure Jerkoff across the way is still available. Though with my luck..."

No, I heard no objections.

I went to the post office to mail grant proposals, essay submissions, other such sundries for Henry, and I slouched from the sight of Mr. Bower. Mr. Bower, my damnable Algebra II teacher, dealing envelopes upon the counter like playing cards. I prayed he wouldn't notice me, but his deck was tall, and the line was short, and soon I'd slumped up to the station beside his. "I just need to send these," I muttered. Mr. Bower's shuffling ceased. "Why look at you!" But, when I turned, he wasn't looking at me. He was looking at the woman manning my station, he was looking at the envelopes she had taken. "You know, I taught for forty years," Bower said, "and I still remember all my students! Like this one here..." He took a closer look at Henry's return address.

"Betty," I said. "Betty Bird."

"Well, tell me, Betty! What's become of you?"

"Actually, I'm getting married."

Mr. Bower was bald, with a face like a burnt-out lightbulb. But it flickered to life now. "Excellent institution! Highly recommend it." He squeezed my hand, his spindly fingers surprisingly firm and warm.

Then other hands were on me. One tapped my shoulder, another pulled at my wrist. I turned, and a tall woman in a jean jacket said, "I rode down the aisle on a palomino! It was the most ecstatic moment of my life!"

The other hand tugged me back toward the counter, from one blue-clad woman to another. "Oh sorry!" The postwoman's eyes matched her uniform. "I just wanted to see the ri-ing! Ooh! *Lovely*."

Prof P also endorsed the ring. It was no longer green and elastic. It was platinum and filigreed, it was an old mine-cut diamond flanked by synthetic sapphires fused sometime midcentury, maybe earlier. It was on my hand and in Prof P's, it was a swift and cold little landscape, suspended for the professor's inspection. "The filigree's quite something..." We were sitting at the kitchen table, waiting for my mother to emerge from the basement with a celebratory bottle. *What will he look like! Where will you meet!* "Interesting shapes... Not overly ornate. Sort of...geologic, actually? Remember *The Enigma of Desire*? You know, *ma mère, ma mère*. Dalí based the central structure on these rock formations near his house..."

In the gallery, I typed the words, *enigma, desire, mother, mother*, compared my ring with the desolate image on Solly's screen. *Engagement ring*, I typed. *Wedding ring*, I typed. Ten million sites flared up from nothing, ten million bodiless voices expressing interest and approbation.

No one objected. Everyone was solicitous, appreciative. So, for the next ten months, I answered every question with the available, the approvable, response.

"When was the last time you had a cleaning?" the dentist wondered.

"Sorry," I answered. "It's just I'm getting married..."

"Is there another card you can try?" the gas station cashier asked.

"Well, actually, I'm getting married, so..."

"Do you have time to participate in a public opinion survey on the current administration," the phone-squawk inquired, "particularly its handling of the ongoing conflict in—"

"Getting married!" said I.

"Betty?" the woman in the makeup aisle murmured. "Betty Bird?"

"No way," I said. "It can't be!"

But it was. Jenny Oeuf, my next-door neighbor freshman year, she of the seesaw stomach. Jenny, who'd fled X when she failed her MCATs, who was running for state senate at the time of our encounter, I'd seen it on my mean screen. I hadn't believed it, but here she was in a powder blue pantsuit, her hair pulled back severely, a lipstick in one hand, a costumey briefcase in the other.

"Jenny! What are you doing here?"

Why, buying lipstick, of course! Could I recommend a flattering shade? I'd always paid attention to such things, hadn't I, and she never had time, especially not these days...

"But what are you doing back in X?"

Jenny grinned an already lipsticked (oh expertly so!) grin. Of all the crazy things, she'd been at the U! Well, she supposed I must pass through campus all the time if I lived here—did I still live here?—but for her it was...*strange*. They'd asked her to be on a panel, 'Seeing Beyond Your Major,' some such thing. Anyway, Jenny, along with several other alumnae who'd pursued careers outside their original areas of study, had been invited to talk to seniors.

"They even videoconferenced Sarah in! She's, like, a movie star now. Did you see *Get Along Home, Betsy, Betsy*? Oh, I *know*. I didn't either! But, yeah, she just got a part in something really major, I guess? I don't really follow that stuff. But remember how she had super short hair in college? Now her hair is *so* long. It was always such a striking red, of course—"

It was dishwater, Jenny, I wanted to say, it was my color on a bad day. Sarah had dyed it red for the remake of *Wife vs. Secretary*, kept it red because that flick was her first little break. Though I had noticed a darker base color in the most recent red-carpet photos... And newish copper highlights that made her skin shimmer like a summer peach... I said this, instead: "Cool!"

"Have you kept in touch with Calliope? We should all, like, get together! Except I'm pretty sure Cal had to get back. You know she's a journalist, right? Mostly print, I guess, but she said she's looking to move into television, cover more foreign policy, given everything that's going on?"

Wrong again, Jen! Calliope wasn't *looking* to move into television, Calliope was *on* television. I'd seen her myself, clenching an outsize AP mic, wrenching her face, Henry-like, until it was almost comically grave. She looked younger than she had in college. And, though, if memory served, she was not quite 5'2", onscreen she looked positively—

"You look great," Jenny said.

"So do you," I answered. It was true, relatively.

"It's good to see you, Betty! What have you been up to? I haven't heard a thing about you since we graduated."

I said my line. And there—ah—something hopeful had been flying about Jenny's mouth, up and through her eyes, until I pulled the trigger on *married*, turned her face to a shot bird. "You're—oh, oh great! I mean, of course, right? Of *course*. But congratulations!" Too late. I'd seen it: Jenny Oeuf, the slick-haired, slickly lipsticked politico, was jealous. "Thanks," I said, elated, ashamed, because Jenny Oeuf envied Betty Bird, and for no reason other than that she would soon be Betty Block. Ridiculous? Yes. Disheartening? Indeed. Yet, even now I remember running through the snow into Henry's arms, and I understand Jenny's jealousy. I know better, but still I find myself wondering: what could be freer than the feeling I had then, caught?

All my life ever since I was a little girl—
What dream could mean more?

15.

One Wednesday when I was seventeen my brother knocked on my bedroom door. "Betty? You have to come. I had an incident."

He led me to the garage, to our father's fender.

"What am I supposed to be seeing?"

He pointed, I squinted: a dent. "I had an *incident*. I—I hit something."

A few days later Danny hit another something while trying to squeeze into a slim space in the library lot. Luckily this something was a maybe-abandoned Toyota, its body already scarred. But the next week he split one wood panel of Mrs. Mitchell's station wagon, while Mitchell, the driver's ed teacher, watched from the high school steps. A few weeks after that, he split another, the entire JV football team as witness.

As the incidents accumulated, we all grew fond of the term. Our parents used it often, in spite of their spiking insurance rates. (Father: "When did the Ministro send that email—you know, perpetual moral rights protections, blah blah blah? Was it before or after Incident #12?" Mother: "Why do they care? The last time anyone even covered *The Creation...* was around Incident #3...") We all appreciated the inconsequence the term lent Danny's crashes. And I appreciated its evocation of my experience, because, soon enough, I'd sat in the passenger seat during the incidence of several incidents.

I was supposed to be schooling my brother in defensive driving, and yet, in his passenger seat, I always fell under some spell. "Turn the music down," I'd remember to say at some point, but, soon enough, the music was up again, and Danny was tapping, tappity-tapping, his hands hitting the steering wheel, his feet thumping the pedals, as the world behind the window fell into rhythm with his song. A curly-tailed dog with a fox's pointy ears pranced, one-two, one-two. A chorus of horns bipped to the beat, three-four. A sports car slowed, its driver shaking an outraged fist, five-six-seven-eight, as he cried, "You're gonna get us all killed someday!"

"Uh-oh," I said. "I think you almost had an incident?"

Little did I know how useful the term would prove years later, during my marriage to Henry.

Have I mentioned my husband's incidents? I—ha ha ha ha hate—have!? Well, that's *strange*! The truth is, I seldom bring them up, uninterested as I am in accepting that, in spite of the career I made of being nothing, I turned into something in the end.

The truth is?

I'm just one more not-so-old woman who got caught in an old, old plot.

16.

Disappointed?

But it's a timeless plot!

No? ...A tired plot?

A plot so old it's new again, then!

Okay, fine, it's not.

A Greckan plot (see: Stone, Matt; Becko, Kai; Wrecko, Rye; Gecko, Coy "Coyote"; et al., infidelitycidents of). A Grecian plot (see: well...Zeus).

A plot so uncool it has to get cool again sometime! A plot so used up the vanguard will need it, the happening kids heed it—even Lizzie'll be eating it up!

No!?

A plot so played out I should apologize then, because I just can't stop playing it through—

17.

Incident #1 came to my attention the night I came back from Amsterdam. That magical snow-twinkly night! When I rushed across the white lawn and into Henry's arms, when I curled into him on the sofa, when I pressed my cheek against his—hard, hard, but not hard enough, oh why were we still two separate beings? "I missed you," I whispered.

"I missed *you*," he whispered back.

"Oh god, you can't know how much I missed you!"

"I can. I do. It seemed like life wasn't *happening* without you here as my witness! There's so much I've wanted to tell you! I kept a list, actually."

Henry's list: *grant, window, roast chicken, Text, weird night at PP, Lover's Discourse, socks*. I listened eagerly, as Henry glossed this outline of two weeks.

So much had happened! He'd won a grant from the F for Film Fund; he'd finally gotten an article accepted for publication in, wait for it, *Text*. *Text*! But, oh, those triumphs seemed incidental in the face of other, truer achievements, the way he stood at his window each and every night, for example, flicking his flashlight three times at *my* dark window.

"But I wasn't there!"

"I kept having these visions where you just never came back and I was an old man suddenly, flicking my stupid flashlight, one-two-three, one-two-three, *I-love-you, I-love-you*."

We kissed.

But, oh, what else, what else!? Henry had gone to Maison Robert and ordered the roast chicken for two. Forty-two dollars just to make himself sick on butter and drippings, sick at how his fantasy had failed him. He'd planned to pretend I was sitting across from him, picking off my own petite pieces of the huge bird, but, oh, it hadn't worked, I wasn't there. My socks were, though! Did I realize I'd left my socks at his place, the black ones with the turquoise stars on the soles? Well, he'd worn them all week, to sleep, to school, to Maison Robert beneath his dress shoes. And, oh yes, he said, glancing at the list, this was practically the best thing, he'd read Barthes's *A Lover's Discourse* for the twelfth time, only to realize that the twelfth was actually the first. How could he have understood readings #1–11, when he had never truly loved?

"What's *weird night at PP*?"

"Oh, exactly! That's exactly what I mean! Whenever anything even moderately interesting happened it was like it hadn't, because I wanted to tell you, but I couldn't."

It was the funniest thing! Henry had stopped in the Book Nook for more Barthes, and he and the girl behind the register got to talking. She *was* a girl, really, fifteen, sixteen, with freckles and a streaky side ponytail, and Henry had been surprised she even knew who Barthes was. He was more surprised still when she scrawled her phone number on his receipt. He called her, of course—

"You called her?"

"Well, that's my policy. I feel like if you put yourself out there like that, it's only right to call. Respectful, you know?"

"Oh." *Oh.*

*Any*way, they met up at Peak Park, Henry, Book Nook, and Book Nook's school chums, Billy, Sally, and Z. They sat together on a bench and watched the sunset; they drank the beer Book Nook had asked Henry to bring. Then Henry professed his profession and the kids started calling him "Teach," asking him to grade them: Z did a cautious cartwheel (A-/B+), Billy polished off Sally's beer in three pulls (B), Book Nook recited "The Lovesong of J. Alfred Prufrock" from memory, and she got an A, because she really, really went for it, stripping down to her underwear so as to make a convincing etherized patient, asking Henry to lie on the ground beside her so she could "speak in the spread-out evening's voice," whispering the poem into his ear. "It was so odd," Henry said. "And I felt so old! I couldn't wait to tell you about it, I was describing it in my mind to you even as it was happening, but then I came home, and you weren't here, and it was...desolating."

He pulled me close, pressed his cold lips to my brow.

Incident #2 occurred not two months later. In spite of countless commissions for variations on *The Creation*..., my mother was finally trying to find her way toward something new, and was loath even to go near the ceiling from which her famous figure stared. So I was at the U, picking up fan mail for her as a favor. I was approaching the Art & Art History Department office when whom should I see but Henry, standing at the end of the hall? Misty, the department secretary, was standing across from him. I quickened my step, switched to a skip. I threw one arm around the befuddled Misty, the other around my betrothed. "My two favorite people!" I said.

Misty was not one of my two favorite people, but I liked her well enough. I hadn't seen her in forever, but I *had* known her since the days I'd stayed after class with Prof P, collecting papers and wheeling the projector back to its alcove in the office. Misty was a petite hatpin of a woman, prone to flushed skin and floral prints.

"Hey!" Henry said, beaming. "You know Miss Misty?"

"I do!"

"I'll let you two talk then. I have to get to class—would that it were not so! I'll see *you* later." Did he actually wink at me? "And, oh, let me know, Misty!"

"You know Professor Block?" Misty asked, once the professor in question had left. "Do you know him well—I mean, *how* do you know him?"

I was just about to utter the favored phrase—*getting married!*—when Misty went on: "Because he just asked me out? I mean, he's very nice, and he's handsome, of course, but I only met him a few minutes ago. *How* do you know him?"

"He asked you out?"

"We were talking about corpse flowers? You know, the *amorphophallus titanum*? They're super rare—they take seven years to bloom, but then the blossom is the largest in the world. Anyway, Professor Block knew all about them! The bloom only lasts for two days, and he said he'd been planning to go too, you know, to the arboretum in Peak Park next week? Supposedly they smell like rotting meat, but are just so dramatic visually! The point is, he said we should go *together...*"

Oh, I said. *Oh.* The thing was, I was pretty sure Professor Block hadn't meant it the way Misty *thought.* Actually, I was *more* than sure he was just being friendly—he was new in town, relatively, and he was *very* friendly. He was my neighbor, actually, and, yes, I did know him, I knew him well, and I well knew he hadn't asked Misty out!

18.

Misty was the last woman to surprise me. After Incident #2, I did the surprising myself.

Cf. Incident #4. I am maneuvering an unwieldy grocery cart around a tight corner, when whom should I see at the end of aisle three, but my beloved Henry? He is holding a head of cabbage, nodding his own sweet head at a woman in red. She wears a long coat with a furry collar, holds a cabbage identical to Henry's.

My cart pulls me along. "Hi," I say.

"Betty!" Henry grins, releases cabbage into cart, puts hand into mine. "What are you doing? I thought *I* was cooking tonight."

The woman in red springs back, moisture springs to her eyes. She does not know me, she will never know me, and yet she hates me and will forevermore.

Or: Incident #6. The setting: Maison Robert. Henry and I have agreed to share the roast chicken this time, to meet at seven, at the bar. I arrive at 7:05. Henry is there already, leaning toward an extremely un-Lizzie-like barmaid. "Sorry I'm late," I say, but it is the barmaid who is sorry. "What's your poison?" she asks as I slide onto the stool beside my dearest love's. I shake my head, because I have no taste for strychnine tonight.

The incidents incidented on. #8 occurred in the home I would soon co-own. I stumbled over after "work," put my hand to the front doorknob, though it was already turning. "Oh!" Maiden #8 cried. "Who are you?"

Henry made the introductions. Eight was Greta Slate, film critic at the *X-aminer*. She was writing a piece on Welles, and, well, she needed to interview Henry. And I? I was the girl next door, if also the imminent inhabitant of this house, Betty Bird, soon-to-be Block.

"Congratulations," Greta said, near-sincere. Even then I knew: if Greta Slate was happy for me, it was because she was not me.

But at least she affected pleasure, at least she tried harder than soon-to-be State Senator Oeuf, who, in the makeup aisle, sharply said, "What did you say his name was?"

"Henry Block."

"You don't mean the professor at the U? I just met him. I thought, I mean, *I* thought...well...never mind what I thought."

"Sorry," I said.

"What are you sorry for? Don't be sorry!" She seemed about to cry. "It's just...it's a funny coincidence, that's all."

No, Jenny: nothing co- about it. It was an incident. A mere moment's interruption to days, weeks, months of romantic happiness, of Henry holding me, in rapt gaze, rippled arms! No, Senator, it was only an incident! Nothing consequential or dangerous, nothing that merited mentioning.

19.

Of course, I *had* mentioned at least one incident to Henry, when he said on the evening in question, "You should come to campus more often. Seriously, just come to work with me from now on! We can team-teach!"

I laughed. Ha! We kissed.

"Incidentally," I said, "Misty thought you were asking her out."

"Misty?" Henry's face clouded, cleared. "That administrative assistant?"

"You asked her to go see a corpse flower with you? I didn't know you were such a naturalist!"

"I'm not really, I just—strange she would take it that way. She just—she seemed—sad." He moved his face around. "I was trying to be friendly."

"That's what I told her."

And what need was there to repeat this circular conversation after Incident #3 or #33 or #63? Anyway, weren't these petty policings beneath me? Henry seemed to think so. Yes, Henry's cocked head, and crooked, confounded look said this: it was embarrassing to be conversant in such rhetoric. Hadn't I trained for something other?

Indeed! In spite of my charmingly old-fashioned name, I was a not-so-old woman whose mother had told her bedtime stories about transhistorical feminist aesthetics and hyperperformance as a means toward gender nihilism! I knew—had ever known!—that social monogamy stemmed from one or another fucked-up cultural process overdue for an undoing; I knew it was just one more means of patrolling and controlling women's bodies, not to mention an all-too-common corruption of the commons! Should people be privatized too!? Ha! How's that for a comment on capitalism, Boyfriend G—Boyfriend H—whoever? Then one night I was winding spaghetti around my fork when my father said, "Who's *that*?" He was looking out the window. He was looking at Henry's house. I turned. And Greta Slate turned Henry's front doorknob once more. Had Greta rung the bell? Had Greta knocked? Not according to my paterfamilias! Even so, she turned that knob and stepped inside.

"Greta Slate," I said. "She's been interviewing Henry about Orson Welles." Then I said the words that should have gone without: "It's nothing."

"Seems like she's made herself at home."

"It's nothing," I repeated.

I repeated the phrase through dinner and dish-washing, through the slow traipse toward Henry's, the slow turning of the knob so recently turned by Ms. Slate. It's nothing nothing nothing. And what did I find within? Nothing! Nothing but my darling Henry tossing aside *A Lover's Discourse*, rising from the couch, rushing to me, embracing me, whisking me into the car and off to a movie, just as we'd planned.

It's nothing, I repeated, as I sunk into my seat, stuffed popcorn into my mouth.

Again I was correct, because the popcorn tasted like nothing, and the movie was about nothing, it starred a nothing-actor and a nothing-actress, who whispered nothing-nothings into each other's numb ears. I blinked against the blank light of the screen, strained to hear the score over my brain's refrain. Nothing nothing nothing nothing nothing. Nothing nothing nothing nothing nothing nothing nothing.

"So?" Henry said on the ride home. "I mean, gorgeous camerawork, right? But wasn't the storytelling a little lackluster? I mean, that scene with her just standing on the terrace seemed to go on forever..." No narrative content! Nothing nothing nothing nothing! "What'd you think?"

"Nothing."

175

"Betty?" He was pressing the gas, we were ascending our hill. "Is something wrong?"

Perhaps I *should* bring up the incidents! Perhaps I *could* talk about them in terms the vanguard would need, the happening kids heed! Perhaps I could play it so cool I'd make this played-out situation cool again!

We pulled into his driveway. "Did Greta stop by tonight?"

"I told you she was coming over. She wanted to watch a couple scenes from *Mr. Arkadin.* Wanted me to provide a sort of director's commentary. Like a DVD extra." He chuckled.

"My dad thought it was kind of, um, odd? You know, that she just walked in. Like, without knocking or ringing the doorbell or anything?"

Nicely done, Betty Bird-Almost-Block! It's your *dad's* problem, your nigh-on elderly *dad* who endows incidents with uncool import, who perceives the nuanced events of these not-so-old times in such circumscribed style!

"Are you crying? Why are you crying?"

Oh.

Oh shit.

And, oh, what the hell?

I told him. Catalogued Incidents #1, #2, #10, my speech so old it was old again, my tone so tired it was simply tired. Yes, I was crying—hard. "I, um, don't really like it sometimes, when I, like *hiccup* have to, you know, explain to, to people I *know*, that you're, um, not, like, asking *them* out, and now my own *gasp* *splutter* *father* im-implies you're, like, *cheating* on me, in, in the middle of din, din, dinner."

I was uncool, undone, but, for a while anyway, Henry was the Henry he'd ever been, eager, studious. He nodded as I spluttered, murmuring interest and understanding. Mm, he said. I see, I think I see. Still, he sought perfect comprehension! "Right," he said, "so,

I'm wondering now, given the way you're framing this, hm... So, okay, does it bother you to know that when I went to that conference in Málaga I slept with a colleague? I'm sorry, I'm sorry..." ha ha ha! "I didn't *sleep* with Lucía, we just shared a bed. We were in her room after a panel, just, you know, batting some ideas about, discussing whether authenticity, or *autenticidad* as Lucía would say, is even a valid term to apply to film, and then it was late and we were tired and we just sort of...fell asleep."

I was spluttering, gasping: I couldn't respond at length. Ye* hiccup*es.

A remarkable remark, *yes*. A terrific term! In that dark car, I answered all of Henry's queries with that slick, quick syllable.

Yes, Henry, it does bother me that you slept in the same bed with a *colleague* just as it bothers me that you exchanged phone numbers with the meter reader dental hygienist visiting scholar high school student have you ever heard of statutory rape by the way just as it *hiccup* bothers me that you made me love you even though I wouldnevercouldnever that you made me into anywomaneverywoman just another woman who loves and loves and says yesyesyesyesyes to love just because you look at her with that wonderfulterrible light in your terriblewonderful eyes just because you look at her and look at her and your look tells her she's there.

Yes.

Yes.

YESYESYESYESYESYESYES, motherfucker!

Through every yes, Henry was Henry, murmurous and thoughtful, flatteringly intent, considerate, considering. He was mming, asking, answering—until suddenly he wasn't.

My hiccups flew about the car, my sniffling stopped up my nose, my sobbing stopped up my eyes, but Henry sat silent, his eyes on his lap. Then he put the key in, turned.

"What are you doing?"

We rolled backward into the street.

"Where are we going?"

We quarter-turned, engine vrooming.

"Henry?"

No answer.

"Henry!"

But Henry was not Henry now. He stared into the windshield as we sped down Scholar and Gown. He stared, his mouth a grim line, as I cried, "What are you doing? Where are we going?"

The hospital was lit up like a gallery. We pulled into the circular drive in front of Urgent Care. Henry turned off the car.

"What are we doing here?" I had stopped crying. "Are *you* crying?"

His snuffling stopped him from answering, but finally Henry said, "I need to go to the hospital. I knew this would happen."

"What do you mean? *What's* happened?" Also, wasn't this a grandmother's move, the mad scene, the best scene, etc.? Shouldn't it have been, oh I don't know, my move?

"You don't love me anymore. And it's just—it's so fucked up—because I *worship* you—" *That's the key, Betty, that's the absolute key!* "You know that, right? Oh god. Something's wrong with me. I need to go to the hospital."

"Stop!" I said. Because, yes, though dry-eyed and grim-mouthed as any Guy-Greco hero, Henry Block was somehow also…crying!? Not to mention plonking his forehead against the steering wheel, punching his temples, pulling his hair.

It went on this way (Henry: "Aaaaegheehehh*splutter*hiccup*aeeeeeee!" Betty: "Sh, sh, stop it…"). In the driveway, I had demanded comfort and instruction, but, in the hospital drive, I comforted, I instructed. And, though I recognized this reversal as unjust, I was also relieved by it. How much better to be unsputtering and sure! How lovely to be removed from the conversation that had undone me, unbecomed me (to say nothing of my mother's supposed legacy)! And how excellent, how unexpectedly exceptional, to know what I had not known only minutes ago, what I'd scarcely known all my life: *what to do.*

Step one: Place hand on Henry's hand, remove hand-the-latter from Henry's hair. Step two: place hand on Henry's shoulder, set said shoulder against seat. Step three: Say, "Sh." Step four: Say, "I do love you." Step five: Say, "Let's go. We don't need to be here." Step six: Take the keys. Step seven: Drive.

20.

For nearly a year, I knew what to do. Move awayawayaway!—way away!—from those awful minutes in the driveway. Undo my undoing. Reverse my unbecoming.

So?—I became.

First, I became Betty Block, standing panicky in City Hall beside Henry, white freesia wilting in my clammy, fretful hands. (You expected a fetching bouquet of corpse flowers, perhaps?) And once I'd become a wife, I became a good wife. Oh, I went to the gallery in the mornings (most mornings...many mornings, anyway), I swift-clicked through a violent confusion of news, then stared at kissing figures misting into Solly's screen until I, too, disappeared. But during the hours I existed? I scrubbed plates until my own scrubbed face blinked back. I scrubbed cupboard faces, counter spaces, floorboards, lathering my way from room to room. I bought carpet cleaner, and scrubbed our aqua pile until it became a frothy soap-sour sea. I took my grandmother's table out of storage, rubbed its antique teak with a Danish oil befitting an authentic Jens Risom. I did loads and loads and loads and loads of laundry—I stain-sprayed, I fabric-softened, I starched Henry's shirts stiff, I mated his socks. I loop-de-looped an iron over his slacks, cursiving my name into khaki, watching *Betty Block* become and unbecome and rebecome. My mother is no cook, nor was my grandmother before her, but I stuffed shelves with recipe books, splattered their pages with those recipes' results. Caneton aux pêche and aux navets and aux cérises. Poulet à la broche or rôti à la Normande. I broiled and baked. I griddled and grilled. For nearly a year, my husband, Henry Block, was thrilled.

But if I was moving away from that unfresh hell in the driveway, what was I moving toward?

21.

This.

It was April, somehow. I had been Betty Block for four months. I had been in the grocery store for no more than four minutes when my phone brrrred. In memory, I know the news is bad before I've fished phone from purse—but did I? I know this: I was rolling through the World Foods aisle when I stopped and said, "Hello?" I was staring at a jar—Isabelita's Aioli, hecho en casa—at a tiny cartoon-lady sporting a giant garlic-bulb hat. "Hello?" I said, but the smiling face didn't answer.

"Eeeeeeeuuuuuuuuugggggghhh."

"Henry?" I knew the sound of his tearless despair.

"Aaaaaaaeeeeeeeuuuuugggghh," he said.

"What did you say?"

"What—what—guhggh—what—would *you* say if, eeeeegguuuuhgheehhhhggggghhhhhh, I told you, aaaaeeeeeoooooggggghhh, I ugggghh, ooouuuggghed someone?"

"What do you mean you 'ooouuuggghed' someone?"

"Eughhheeeghghh."

"And what do you mean 'if'? Did you or didn't you?"

"Eggggh, egggh, ugggghh...ugggghh."

Already, I was crying. My garlic-hatted gemela looked back at me, uncomprehending. ¡Someone get Isabelita a translator, por favor!

"Who?" I said. ¿Quién?

"Does that, aaaaeeeeggghhh, matter?" Henry answered.

Yes and no. But did the answer to my next question matter? To that I offer a quick slick syllable: Sí. ¡SÍ SÍ SÍ SÍ SÍ, hijo de puta!

The question: "Are you saying you slept with this person?"

Henry's answer, with the vowel sounds edited out: "Yes and no."

"You mean you just slept in the same bed—" la misma cama "—like last time?"

Isabelita and I stared at each other. There was no need to translate Henry's response. The word is the same in both languages.

22.

First I became a wife, then I became a good wife, then I became a mommy. Have I mentioned this last stage?

No!?

Ha! ...I meant to say *mummy*. No need to be an *id*iot, after all—no need to bring a baby into this!

Moving away, away, way away having failed, I tried, instead, to stay still. I tried, I succeeded, I stayed still in bed for eight days straight. What I'd once hoped would be a new room with new things, beautiful things for a new beautiful life, became tall and small—a mausoleum. Those piles of dimes on the desk? Why, those were for Charon, those would buy my passage to the underworld! Soon, they would float across the room, soon they would fall, light and cold, upon my eyes. O why not sing of that ultimate wander? Perhaps all the nothing-nothing I'd practiced over the years had been leading me somewhere epic after all! I could feel my stomach chewing on itself.

But I had a problem. My heart beat on, and I could not even seal up my mausoleum. Henry was somewhere near, one room over or under, pacing the halls, his voice in the walls. He seemed to be talking on the phone... But to whom? The someone he'd ooouuuggghed, perhaps? That special someone who had to be about fourteen, judging by all the after-school hours she spent gabbing on her Nokia? And what tale was Henry telling her this time, what epic was he making out of the materials of his life, out of me, his mummy-wife? Was he singing a song about a good or bad man? Was he saying words I'd heard and heard? Whatever the content, his tone was intently sober, intently somber, and utterly, utterly content. Yes, whatever story my husband was spinning, one thing was clear enough: *Henry Block: A Biopic!* had reached its enrapturing climax.

I got up eventually.

I couldn't just let him enjoy it.

23.

I got up and I got out and I got in again. I got into Henry's car and sunk into the all-too-familiar depths of his passenger seat. Then I got up and I got out and I got in again, slinking through a gray hallway that smelled, funereally, of flowers, though the only flowers grew up the quiet carpet, up, up, through two gray doors. Doors through which I was slinking until, at long last, I was sinking, into the unfamiliar depths of Dr. Allegra Crouch's couch.

Henry wouldn't stop talking in his biopic voice. He perched on the next cushion, said with intense solemnity, "Thank you so much for seeing us."

Dr. Crouch looked at each of us in turn. "Is this your first time in couples therapy?"

Henry answered at some length: Why couples therapy, yes, though he himself had been analyzed, medicated, demedicated, remedicated.

My own answer was slick, quick: "Yes."

Dr. Allegra Crouch wore a straight gray skirt, a belted gray jacket—alpaca, maybe? Her eyes were squinty, as if ever appraising. "Why don't you tell me a little more about what's brought you here?"

As Henry answered, conversing with impressive facility in all manner of a-la-mode rhetoric, expressing a desire to "collaborate" more with me on "cogent, but flexible, relational boundaries" that "honored" the "spectrum" upon which our "idiosyncratic preferences" might lie, as he began to *eggggh* and then *uggghh*, I watched Dr. Crouch. She had beautiful, complicated hair. Yellow-white and braided, like an Irish knit. As Henry *neeeggghhed*, she nodded. From time to time, she caught my eye, smiled slightly.

"I'd like to hear both your voices today," she said at one point.

Henry answered, "Exactly! That's *exactly* why we're here! In a sense, that's where these misunderstandings arise, out of a failure to *collaborate*. I need Betty to be clearer about *her* needs so that we can do better *work* together, as a couple, in the future. But, I guess, well, yeah, I mean, like you're suggesting, Doctor, I guess I need Betty to, um, articulate some empathy, or, uh, *forgive me*, to use an antiquated phrase, first of all? I mean how can we move forward if she refuses to do that?"

Dr. Crouch tipped her chin toward me, her squint turning inquisitive. "How do you feel hearing Henry say that, Betty?"

"Um..."

"Do you feel capable of 'forgiveness'?"

That trick syllable hadn't failed me yet. Anyway, I said it: "Yes."

"We're out of time," Dr. Crouch answered. "But I'd like to take this conversation up again. With each of you independently, if that sounds all right? I think it might make sense for each of you to come in for your own establishing session?"

All week, I looked forward to independence, imagining Dr. Crouch and me in her pigeon-colored office, nodding at one another, smiling just slightly, radiating cautious understanding.

We wore identical alpaca jackets, identical straight skirts. I tilted my eyes toward the ceiling as I told my alpacaed pal just how I'd gotten here, starting with the snow-starry night, Henry and I running toward one another over the unspoiled ground, smash-crash, before moving backwards to my mother, my grandmother...

But when the day came, I was only a few words into my script when Dr. Crouch nodded at the box of Kleenex on the coffee table.

"Take your time," she said.

Time. The clock turned without seeming to. I wiped my eyes, cleared my throat; watched the second hand spin unticking, pull the minute hand imperceptibly along. I flapped my hands, panicky. I was supposed to be moving backwards, into the past and past it, but I kept sinking into the snow in the first scene, my voice slipping on a single word, its variations. *Henry*, I kept repeating. *Ha—he—he. It's just that he—hee hee—him, Henry. Ha,* I laughed? *Ha ha ha ha. H-Henry, I—hey hey.* What word was I trying to find?

I took another Kleenex. Then another two or ten. Dr. Crouch was talking now, explaining the link between clinical depression and...

"Rumination. Dwelling, brooding...passively focusing on symptoms of distress, on its causes or results? You might think it will help you move forward, understand the problem, find a solution, but unfortunately it's been proven to perpetuate anxiety, to *produce* despair." She blinked, patted her intricate hair, hands *sh sh*-ing against her tresses. "And it—rumination, I mean, depressive rumination—occurs most often in women, especially those with excessive relational focus. That is, a tendency to overvalue relationships to such an extent as to sacrifice identity, self... And it's been linked to other injurious behaviors... Eating disorders... Binge drinking..." She blinked again: an intensified squint. "I bring this up because if you *have* in fact chosen to 'forgive' your partner, a tendency to ruminate may prove a serious impediment..."

You must think of the future, dear, not the past!

Dr. Crouch cleared her throat, raised her volume a notch. "An impediment that, in addition to interfering with efforts to achieve your stated goal, might even lead to further trauma."

"Oh," I said. *Oh.*

The doctor offered her slender smile. "How does what I'm saying make you feel? Given that," she prompted, "you've stated both that you wish to 'forgive' and that you feel fixated on these 'incidents,' this last one in particular?"

I looked down at my lap. It was cluttered with crumpled Kleenex.

"Betty?"

"You're saying that if I want to forgive my, uh, Henry, I should just, like, think about something else?"

Dr. Crouch's forehead was braided to match her hair. "Well... *if* you do wish to 'forgive'—perhaps. Distraction *has* been proved to counteract rumination. In fact, studies have shown that directing a ruminator to think about something as simple as the layout of a room, say, can markedly, if temporarily, decrease rumination as well as self-blame."

I moved my eyes about Dr. Crouch's office—from diploma-wall to Kleenex-table—or, no—no, what was it called? For a good minute I searched for the word, and thought about nothing but her table, I swear.

24.

Coffee-. Console-. Sofa-. Side-. For some time, I contemplated tables. For some time, I drew mental floorplans of every room I entered, configured the furniture, considered the flow. Gondola sofa. Aqua pile. That ancestral dining T—Jens Risom original or no. The TV opening the wall like a window onto my parents' house—*worship is the key, the absolute key*—Orson the Man's balletic hands turning a different key into a coin. Henry's eyelids drooping, as if he were hypnotized by the man on the screen in his magician's clothes, by his famed baritone drone. Decommissioned even, so why not go, why not attend to the speedometer's swift glow? To the L-O-N-E-S-O-M-E woman switching on in the sky? Though I'd driven that stretch countless times it was only in that therapeutic period that I noticed her, all credit due to Allegra Crouch. Because I was doing as the good doctor ordered, thinking about something as simple as the layout of the B-A-L-L-R-O-O-M. Porthole, bar, black back hall, Goodman's table turning to my grandmother's, turning to Goodman's again. Scarred barwood, antique teak. Those mean clean lines, that long strong grain—I swear I was thinking about tables.

And at some point during this period, I was so distracted, so well directed, that I casually dropped that antiquated phrase, *I forgive you.*

I promise, I might have said, *what's past is paaaaaaghst. You must think of the future, dear!*

In that case, Henry just knew he'd love, or we'd love a baby, so, yeah, seriously, why not get a dog or son? We didn't have to start *trying* yet, but we could start charting, bring a hobby into this? I checked my discharge, made checkmarks on our calendar, kept eating processed meats and unpasteurized cheeses, kept drinking the Old Fashioneds that appeared unbidden before me, but at least I avoided aioli, aioli, aioli, aioli, aioli, flipped past soap operas ("All my life ever since I was a little girl—"), telenovelas ("¡—siempre he tenido el mismo sueño!"), so that I might consider the Westminster Dog Show, why not? Round of a-paws, please! Going to the breeder with my husband didn't mean I was one. Going to the humane society with H didn't mean adding another H (U-M-A-N) to our society. It meant staying distracted. It meant staying.

So why not take in our landscape from the porch, attending to line, texture, color, and form, of course? Why not process down the steps, from hardscape to softscape? Why not release a Frisbee across the green, green grass? And what do you know? I flung, and our new baby fetched. Then I sat and cut and chewed, or at least dropped the unchewed scraps to the furry ground. I was concentrating on something as simple as the layout, fork to the left, knife to the right, yes, I swear I was looking at my plate, admiring the varnish on the duck aux pêche or aux épices or aux navets or aux cérises or aux olives or aux pruneaux or aux raisins or aux raisins blonds or au citron vert or aux mandarines or aux petits pois or aux truffes or au champagne or à la presse or à la choucroute or à la Normande or, fine, fine, fine, fine, fine, fine, fine, à l'orange, why not?

The duck was every bit as delicious as Henry's performance implied, though my portion was a little salty, and a little damp, and fine, fine—

Fine, fine, fine, fine, fine, fine, fine, fine, *fine*—

I was crying, and don't you see why?

Don't you see why I cried as I smashed my chair in, crashed the car door shut? Why I cried as the houses blinked, as the porthole winked? You must understand why I wiped my eyes, pushed vicious fists into them before pushing into the bar, making my bleary way to Goodman's table? It was only Tuesday, nothing to get worked up about! He was talking about the tube amps built into his great-uncle's great room—fucking sweet, because what could be more distracting? Close your eyes, Betty, picture the mean clean lines of that good man's midcentury layout. No, don't open them, don't open them, don't—

"Betty?" Goodman leaned across table, and I was thinking about it, I swear. "Are you—"

Yes!

YESYESYESYESYESYESYES, motherfucker!

Of course I was crying and also trying not to cry. Trying, crying, as I told what was supposed to be a dog story, trying to make like Homer just moved me when I recited the ancient line, *If you could only see the dog as he was when—*

Of course I cried as Lizzie's eyes t-shirt arm zoomed toward me, as I saw what I was about to do, saw I'd done it, saw that zesty puddle. Cried, cried as the barmaid plucked upchucked duck from my hair. What better place to cry than a busted barroom's backhall bathroom? What simpler layout?—scrawled-over mirror, rusted sink—but I digress because yes, I fucking cried, and we all know why. I cried because I never ever drive.

And then my tears were blurring the treetops, making the windshield whirl. I could barely see, the numbers like windy pages—forty, forty-ugh—and then a house was twirling up as if from childhood. Whirl-blurring, doubling, until it was a new house with new things for a new beautiful life, the house next door, the house I shared with Henry—

25.

I came to at the end of the driveway. Yes, one minute my screen was spinning, our beautiful home hurling toward me—gondola sofa, aqua pile, ancestral table, I would smash it all—but the next, I'd flashed to some still scene inside my childhood. Cue the motherfucking harp! Because the grape arbor my father had planted when I was four crept blurrily up the garage, fluttered its festive green hands. Hello, Betty! It was as if we had gone, my family, on a long trip—I was asleep and then I wasn't, falling in one place, waking right here, my father hovering, reaching, soon he'd pick me up and carry me inside.

I blinked. Slept, woke up again. His face floated in the window, a fuzzy moon. Yes, Dad? Are we there yet? Are we back?

He didn't open the door. It was locked, I'd find out later. But he was nodding, speaking, some muffled affirmation: *back*, yes, that's right, *reverse*. "Shift," he said, "shift into reverse!"

My eyes shifted from his face to the waving leaves, then stuck on the wooden garden stake he'd shoved in the soil to mark the driveway's edge. The stake was splintered, slanted; I'd hit it. Which meant I hadn't hit the house that contained my marriage table marriage bed marriage—

Still.

I'd flattened my father's impatiens, bumped his viburnum shrub, and he was sure to scold me soon.

How old are you, Betty?

Last night in the single digits, Dad!

How spoiled are you, Betty?

But, no, my father didn't take my name in vain.

He took this one, instead.

"Orson," he said. "Orson, Orson!" loud now, rapping the glass. "It's Orson. Listen! Wake up! You ran over Orson!"

26.

Disappointed?

But for once there's no need to cut to a scene from *Sweatpoison*! No need to cut to Kai Becko, staggering in a tragic zigzag from Bea's Airstream. Where's Timmy, that sweet son turned levitating demon? And what kind of mother—? But there's no need to ask the questions that contort our hero's face, no need to jump-cut from that face to Becko's clenched and bleeding hands, no need to zoom in as those hands begin to tremble, no need to swing the camera tremblingly to the image that has caused the hero's latest climactic upset. There's no need to cue who else but Frank Sinatra, decibels rising inexcusably as the frame closes in on a bleeding rabbit, on the noose that circles its neck (Fluffhead? But, no—*this* bunny is all too real...). No need to note what a terrific and terrible metronome the dead critter makes, no need to cut to any scene conjured by the mad mind of Guy Greco, because somehow I've conjured my own climactic animal.

Cut to my father's car then, as we speed down the hill, my eyelids squeezing out a single tear. They are squeezing out the sight of Orson's tail, anyway—what's so different about it? It isn't limp, exactly, but soft, somehow...

No, don't look, Betty. Don't look at the dog in your lap. Slam the door, shut the drawer, don't look at his dry snout, don't note its awful, almost artful-seeming stasis. Don't look at the blood on the seatbelt, the blood on the seat cushion, the blood on the armrest, the blood smearing the door. Open your eyes only when your father reappears, a blurry actor in the glass, his muted mouth telling you to get out, yes, you're there yet.

And then we are facing the receptionist across the counter, an old snowflake of a lady with fuzzy hair. "Name?" she says.

"Bird," my father answers.

"It's a bird?"

"Oh sorry," my father says. "That's our name. Jack and Betty Bird."

"And the dog?" Snowflake says. "What's the dog's name?"

She looks in my direction, but no, I will not look down with her at the heaving heap in my arms, will not take his only name in vain. Snowflake smiles as if I've answered, her fingers sleeting across a keyboard. "Or-son. Or-son Bi-ird." Then she is looking up, saying, "Funny name for a dog!" And a wet weight lifts from my arms, and she is steering my father toward a man in white, steering me toward a bright back hallway, where she deposits me on a bench.

The walls are freshly painted, the linoleum agleam. But the most important feature of that final hallway, as I see it now anyway, is the ceiling. This one is empty of ethereal figures—no mothers

here, no gods or sons—the invisibility of its iconography inviolable—but when I close my eyes—when I tilt my head back—when I count to ten and then lift my lids again—at last I see...
Fluorescence...
A wild brightness...
A buzzing, confident...
Light!
Or should I be so bold as to use the definite article?
Why not? Lizzie's not listening, Guy and Goodman and Sunshine never were, but I have to tell myself something.
So?
On the night in question, I saw the light.
Then, in the middle of it: my father's face.

27.

"He's okay except for his left hind leg," Dad said. He sighed, sat. "You got him pretty good there, but they don't think it will actually take that long..."

Don't look, I had told myself, don't look lest you—

But that didn't mean I hadn't begun in not so many months to do as Henry just knew I would. Whether it was good for me or not, I fell like always, and now I loved Orson, loved him. His jaws around my hand, teeth gentle on my skin, as he seemed to lead me, crying, to bed. The damp nose in my neck once I lay down. The sweet silty eyes, so troublingly human, as kind as a mother's or a child's. But don't look, Betty.

And I didn't. Didn't care to observe that Orson had taken to departing the house whenever I did—if the woman was too careless to take care of him—if she was going to fly off, cry off to the Lonesome—fine, fair enough, but he was going to leave too. He was going out to the yard, then the yard's farthest edge, then the driveway, then that other, better driveway, my parents'. My parents aren't dog people, but their unwilled indifference to his species-in-general seemed to relieve Orson; it was preferable, at least, to my willful inattention to him-in-particular. *Herrrrrrrrr? Even herrrrrrrrr?* He lay down, trained his eyes on my distant windshield as I reversed, or as I—

No, don't look, don't look—

And I hadn't, but now, when I looked at my father, when I said sorry sorry sorry like a fucking girl, I more than meant it, I swear.

Here's the thing, though. For the first time in what seemed a long time, I wasn't crying. And I knew exactly how I'd gotten here.

"Well," I said, after a while. "I guess I'd better go tell Henry I ran over his dog."

My father and I smiled at each other.

"Yeah," he said, "tell him."

Tell him!

Tell him!

Tell him!

28.

The truth is the mise-en-scène was right out of a Guy Greco flick. The ceiling panels buzzing down at the linoleum, the bright white-walled hall in between. It gave the whole setup an overexposed aspect, made my father look grizzled as he filled the frame, white stubble poking and glinting. To say nothing of the easy listening that floated from secret speakers in the ceiling. To say nothing of the horrors no doubt occurring behind the long line of doors. But if I were a filmmaker, I'd ignore these aesthetic cues. I'd start the scene in black-and-white, put myself in a silver gown.

I know, I know. But can't I have what I've always wished for, now that I'm trying so hard to get you what you need?

Picture it.

Our heroine sees the light, then tilts her head as if she hears something. What could it be? Her dog moaning as a knife floats close? The sweet synthetic ballad that lilts down from the panels? No. The hospital's eerie sound system has cut out. Our heroine listens to a distant, private song.

She stands.

She taps her foot.

Taps out a swinging rhythm on the square.

And then—what's this? Our heroine is looking down, looking at her dancing feet, the camera telling us to see what she sees. Tap-tap tappity tap-tap. One more tap and the tile...

Turns on!

Yes, the flecks in that single square of linoleum are flickering like filaments, some strange switch willed up, spotlights shining from above and below.

And then? The tile just beyond it lights up too.

Then the next square and the next, click, flick, the fifth tile flicks on, the sixth, the seventh. The eighth! And then another, and another. The next square flares silver, then the next and the next, choreographing a path down the hall.

"Tell him," a man behind her sings—her father, we realize, a minor character. And then the receptionist is back, a snowflake swirling sweetly down the hall, repeating the chorus, "Tell him, tell him."

Our heroine taps forward, stops. Then, a-one, and a-two, and a-one, two, three, four—the doors open, and a white-coated chorus shimmies out, shuffle-stepping one-two, two-two, kick-ball-change, singing, Tell him!

And a-five, and a-six, and a-seven, and an-eight—it's time for the climactic animals! A cat with a bandage strapping down one ear, the other tilting in the jaunty manner of a bowler hat. A chasséing chinchilla, whiskers like a wide bowtie, twin bite wounds brightening its ears. A pandemonium of one-winged

193

parakeets, half-flying, half-falling, the scene shifting into Technicolor. Chartreuse, pineapple yellow, the brightest, most beauteous blue. The tapping ingénue's sequins shimmer in time with the tumorous turtles who shuffle-time-step at her side, shells agleam. She sways along with sneezing yet jazz-ears-ing rabbits, wheezing yet tail-tapping ferrets, with sick mice, rats, hamsters, hedgehogs—

And dogs.

Ta-da!—dogs.

Dogs in casts and dogs in cones. Dogs with bleeding ears, swollen ears, missing ears. Tailless dogs and dogs whose tails bend at the wildest angles. Dogs who vomit in rhythm with the music, whose volume is rising, rising. Tell him! Tell him! Owwwww-rrrooooooooooooooooooooooooooooo! That must be a cue. Because, no matter how mangled, the dogs stand. Yes, those dogs and cats and rodents and vets form a shoulder-height chorus line behind the ingénue. They howl, they meow, they squeal. Tell him, tell him! And then they brush-brush-toe-heel, brush-brush-toe-heel, kick, kick, kick, kick!

And our girl is whirling toward the door that is twirling like a delirious dance partner at the end of the hall. She extends her hands—palms out, fingers splayed. Jazz hands, jazz hands all the way to the exit!

She is halfway there when someone new comes into the frame. A man, of course, dapper in his long white dinner jacket. "Orson?" he says. "Orson Bird?" His eyes are giant stars.

"Betty!"

"Betty Bird, though, right?"

She says yes, even though that isn't her name, exactly.

"You'll save your dog's life if you okay an amputation."

And she does what she always does, sings her favored word one final time, so that the starry-eyed man can close our song by shaking her hand.

"You're a hero," he says. "You're a hero, Betty Bird."

29.

That hallway climaxed in a revolving door, a shushing whoosh. Outside, the night hummed with quiet.

He answered on the third ring, "Beeeeeggghhhh-y!? Whaaagghh? Whaggghhht is it?"

Was I crying again?

No. I was making a sound that was like crying, though—half-spasm, half-song—a sound I'd made before. But it had a new ring. A true ring. Like this:

Ha!

"Hahahenry?" I laughed. "I'm afraid there's been—an incident! And Henry—? Hahaha*hen*ry! The truth is—"

Unidentified photographer
The Beatles Concert—Manchester, 1963
Gelatin silver print, 42.3 x 39.3 cm / 16.7 x 15.5 in

A
HOW I GOT HERE

1.

Picture the past one last time. Picture X in 1986.

I wake up late, mean sun spilling in from the hall. I am sweating. No school today, but I am panicky anyway, up before I've told myself to get up. My room is messy. Drawers disgorge dresses and skirts and nightgowns and tights... A pile of laundry sits humped in one corner. I put on a waistless pink sundress, embroidered at the neck with blue triangles.

Dresses, skirts, nightgowns... But I can't find a single pair of underwear.

I find Danny in the basement playroom. I've followed his voice, clumping downstairs, my bare feet slick, imagining the joke I'll make of his talk. Saturday, 11:30, my mother no doubt in her studio, sketching yet another study of her arm, my father in the adjacent office, drafting another brief on her behalf. I know that no one else is down here.

But there is someone. Mike Updike, an older boy, an only child; he lived on our street just that one year. His mother had nut-colored eyes, long fingers, dark curly hair that fell and fell. She wore ripped jeans and tarnished silver rings.

My brother and Mike Updike are stacking Legos. Neither one looks up, and I wait, I watch. When Danny and I play Legos it isn't like this; we don't just silently build. We make the same-faced Lego-men differentiate themselves, we make them speak in wild voices, helium-high then booming, choked. Our smiling men talk on for hours, the cities they might have inhabited lying in bright pointed pieces at their feet.

I don't know how long I've been standing here, my sweaty skin suddenly cold. I don't know why I feel like crying, why I feel furious at the fluorescence that falls from the ceiling. And I don't know why I'm so mad at Mike Updike, with his neat navy clothes, his leaning eyelashes, his mother's cool drifting from him like a mist. I just know that I want him—not them, but him—to look at me. I want that. And I know exactly what to do.

2.

Have we arrived at the Bettian ur-scene?

3.

I don't remember lifting my dress. I just remember the feeling of air against me, admonitory; raw and rimy, in spite of the heat. "Look," I said. I didn't want both of them to do it—but they did, they lifted their eyes. And even as shame filled me, even as I dropped the dress, as I turned and ran, I also felt a frisson of triumph, the quick flick of rugburn or static shock—the satisfaction that comes with certain knowledge, with being proven right.

Upstairs, I was hot again, and something rotten was moving through my stomach. I curled up on top of my messy bed, tried to convince myself I hadn't done it. It was too fast, I decided. They couldn't have seen.

But then Danny was in the doorway, his eyes huge. Mike Updike was gone, but Danny was there, saying, "Why'd you do that, Betty?" His voice was kind enough, but it was also clotted with awe, and I wanted to slap him across the face.

"Why'd you do that?"

I couldn't tell him why, even as I couldn't stop seeing the scene I'd just occupied. It seemed clipped from a movie—one I'd long known existed, one I already knew by heart, even though I wasn't old enough to have seen it.

But I couldn't say that to Danny, just as I couldn't say I'd thought about Mike Updike before that morning. How to explain that I'd imagined Mike Updike at those windows—my bedroom windows!—his thin body floating up from the lawn, his still face at the glass, watching me, assessing me, as I undressed? Watching and assessing as I undressed and pretended innocence, indifference. I'd had the fantasy again and again. I was only seven years old.

"Why?" Danny repeated. "Why'd you do that?"

I shook my head. "Don't tell," I said.

4.

Have we arrived, at last? Have we gone back, back, back in order to find the scene that might merit a song, or start some sort of story?

It's a beginning, anyway. Now here's the end.

5.

On the sidewalk in front of the animal hospital, I found the word I was looking for. Hate. Ha ha ha hate. I hate you, Henry. I hate—

When I'd said it enough, I smashed my phone shut.

Then? I crashed it open.

E answered on the first ring. It was as if she'd been lying in bed, watching the ceiling spin, waiting for me to call.

"E?" I said. "I have to tell you something—"

"E?" I said. "The truth is—"

6.

And then?

Like a good hero, I fled. Five minutes northeast, 175 miles southwest. You might say I was in desperate, restless motion at last. Anyway, I was begging my father to drive me to E's latest half-house, Orson bandaged up and in my lap again, and the next day I was pleading with E to drive the dog and me to the one true city, to Thirtieth and First, where I knew she was still paying rent.

"How can I ever thank you?" I asked.

"Oh, please!" *Don't be such a fucking girl.* "It's impossible to find a good subletter in this ginormous frat house of a neighborhood!"

We laughed, she left. And then?

Like a good hero, I wandered. To Gristedes and Food Emporium and Fairway. To one or another of the one true's endlessly replicating Duane Reades. I filled E's refrigerator, filled E's medicine chest. I wandered and was lost—water all around me, water on every side—but I got my bearings by seeking the same shabby pizza place for seven nights straight, by ordering the same crisp slice. Then? Action! I went to the donut shop, even though they delivered. I went to the bra emporium, where I was elated (why?) to learn that, with the proper band, I was actually a D cup. And, with Orson, I went to Patsy's Pet Clinic.

On the outside, it looked like a strip club, its storefront curtained in dark velvet, a neon kitten winking through the plateglass; but, inside, a wee, white-coated woman, hair styled like a Shih

Tzu's and tied back with a bitty bow, removed my dog's sutures. "Wound care," she said. "Pain management."

Then she asked me the question, and I said I was all right.

"Aw, I'm sure I have some Kleenex somewhere…" She rummaged around. "You should know, honey, for the dog, it's just a normal thing. It's harder for you… And at home you won't even need the harness."

Home? Like a good hero, I had traveled far from there, but, fine, fair enough, I walked the three blocks back to E's. I fitted a plastic cone around Orson's head. I took it off when his breathing slowed. The incision was far longer than the four inches the dapper dog-doctor back in X had promised, but no matter! It was just a normal thing, right? Normal as a shot-up Komodo dragon, a hanged hare, a twelve-point buck crushed beneath an ice cream truck. My climactic animal's skin was a sick gray-pink where it had been shaved. He wouldn't look me in the eye, seemed too weak to inch toward me. I leaned in, applied the hydrogen peroxide and antibiotic ointment. His tail curled under as if to substitute for the lost limb. "Don't do that," I whispered, "please?" I pressed a cold compress to his torn, sewn flesh. Don't look, I thought, don't look lest—

But then I made myself. There was yellow discharge, an enormous and oddly beautiful bruise.

I slept next to him. I didn't sleep. I took him out to the street so he could crouch, abjectly, beside a flowering bush. When the sutures were out, he began to hop ahead, without my help.

7.

What I'm saying is: I did Odysseus one better. I took the dog, and then? I took care of him. Compress, ointment, cone, leash. Just like that, Orson was almost as he'd been before the incident, *so strong and swift you'd be amazed*! He was pulling me down First to the East Village. He was pulling me up to the Upper East Side. We sailed past a nail salon and a nail lounge. A blowout bar. A waxing "club" a mere six blocks from a waxing "center." Past the General Federal Republic of Germany, past Papua New Guinea, the Republic of Belarus—their consulates, anyway. We crossed the city on 68th, and 53rd, on 10th, on Christopher. Orson's gait was syncopated, snagging, counting off some swinging new song—a-one, a-two, a-one-two-three!

We were on Houston when I saw it, a glowing sign dropped out of the darkness: *How to Marry a Millionaire*. But was this sign a sign? I tied Orson to a leaning tree, jaunted across the sidewalk, a-one and a-two, following a soft spill of light. In the theater's window, there was another sign: "We're Hiring."

"Do you have any experience?" a girl with magenta hair asked. Her pierced tongue flashed meanly. She chewed a knotted wad of blue gum.

A child could have done the work—give Orson an additional limb and some opposable thumbs and he would have excelled in my position! Still, it wasn't a ludicrous question in that city, at that time. "I'm going to grad school," I said. "I've written for *Text*?" I didn't feel like I was lying.

"Who's your favorite director?"

"Orson," I said.

"Good answer."

I worked the 11–7, the 2–10. I served Diet Coke in giant cups to trim gray men with trim gray beards. I pushed a broom down a long smooth slide. I perched on a counter next to Kevin, a freckle-faced senior at NYU. "Shouldn't you, like, be a TA or something?" he asked. Kevin loved Teshigahara, hated the "predictable" Kurosawa. "That's what I'm gonna write my thesis on. It's gonna be, like, an anti-Kurosawa screed." I stood in the dark space between the theater door and a thick red curtain. I listened to the people on the other side, their sighing breath, their ticking brains, their sticky fingers filing through popcorn. I watched movies shine in through the velvet, their light rearranging the linoleum.

8.

Kevin usually mused on the month's movies for the newsletter, but in May he had finals, and I took over. "You sure you got it?" His mouth roiled with gummy worms.

"Totally. *Gaslight* is one of my faves."

"Ha! Nice! People are starting to throw that shit around, though... It's not *gaslighting* unless someone's actually messing with your butane, you know?"

"Totally," I said. "Let's educate these idiots!"

He ha-ha-ed, high-fived me, handed over a DVD in cloudy plastic. "In case you need to cram."

E had a wall-mounted television in an upper corner of her bedroom, so the film fell down from on high. I forgot time, forgot, for a while, where I was, when I was. For a while, E's one true frat house of a neighborhood might have been an hour south of Hollywood, that dim, messy bed my dead grandmother's. I might have been lying beside her, watching her watch Ingrid Bergman clutch hands to breast, then reach into nothing, then sing. How had she gotten there? Why hadn't I asked? And why hadn't I been able to come up with any better—or worse—answer than the scene that fell from the screen?

You must think of the future, dear!

So Maestro Guardi was saying, even as I disobeyed, pressed Rewind, watched the first sequence again. Then I flipped to and fro through the frames, with little regard for the arc.

Orson put his paws on me, fitted his jaw to my thigh, as Bergman sat in the audience, her face wavering from terror to despair, a pianist's fingers quavering on the keys. Hers was an ingénue's face, and also the face of a woman in a car chase or car crash, and, oh, why didn't I—

You must think of the future, dear!

I Paused. Adjusted the dog on my legs to make room for my laptop.

When Paula Alquist (Ingrid Bergman)'s singing teacher exhorts her to "free herself from the past," I wrote, *he seems, at surface, to be encouraging her to embrace her romance with Gregory Anton (Charles Boyer), and, in so doing, a familiar narrative mode—a marriage plot characterized by inciting romantic tension and ultimate romantic resolution. At the same time, his instruction to Paula to abandon her operatic training might be read as an injunction to move beyond the conventional dramatic and romantic storytelling associated with the operatic form, a mode made up by men and dependent upon male musicians: the composer, the maestro, even the accompanist, who, in the first scene of this odd and exciting film, is none other than the heroine's lover.*

"If you are not continuing the lesson," the lover-accompanist says to Paula's teacher in response to the instruction that opens the movie, *"I should like to be excused." This foregrounding of the romantic lead's departure—this casting of him into the film's "past" and out of its immediate "future" just as the heroine is encouraged to abandon her study of an inflexible and patriarchal form—is significant. It will be followed by many others throughout the film—departures that will leave our heroine alone in frame after frame, without apparent dramatic partner. In other words, the heroine will be freed from the past's dominant narrative strategies: she will be left alone with her mind—in silence, without hero or script—but still expected to engage the viewer, to perform and provide dramatic action, narrative content.*

I picked up the remote, pressed Play. Stilled the screen when Bergman fell upon the fainting couch, flipping, flopping, Charlotte Brontë's *Villette* her only scenemate, her gaze flitting about before the gaslights even began flickering. I had always loved this part. It made my heart ting-ting.

In this way, Gaslight *could even be seen as a precursor to the work of artists like Cindy Sherman, and to a postmodern feminist filmmaking tradition typified by Chantal Akerman's* Jeanne Dielman, 23, quai du Commerce, 1080 Bruxelles. *Indeed, years before Akerman's Jeanne will be activated by a sudden and unprecedented lack of domestic activity, Paula reveals the narrative—and even climactic—potential of a woman left isolated in a scene without the distraction or protection of action.*

I depressed Pause, and Bergman leapt up, moving about the room like a caged creature. Orson *herrrrrrrrr*ed as if in response, jumped from the bed as if inviting me to follow. I walked to the window, lifted the blinds on a flickering filmstrip of siren light.

In the time and space of this film—as in our time, our world—it would be unsafe for the feminine subject to be a flâneur (flâneuse?). But she can pace her domestic space, ruminating, thoughts rocketing across her face and distorting her ingénue's visage. Significantly, Bergman's most memorable pacing—and the mental action that movement represents—comes just after her premature departure from a classical recital; it is as if her surprising solitary actions serve as a rejoinder to the unsurprising musical and dramatic structures/strictures she received in the concert hall, underscoring the film's temporary rejection of traditional narrative tactics. The sequence that follows is one of fugue-like intensity, and yet it is formless by conventional dramatic standards. Though our heroine has been robbed of her power not only to act but to clear-sightedly interpret the actions of those around her, this sequence's unfixed form gives her implicit agency, revealing that a dramatic climax can depend on a necessarily passive heroine, requiring no actors or action at all. Indeed, the film disappoints only when conventional plotting intercedes, implying a resolution to the heroine's problems that the true, languorous climax satisfyingly and movingly challenges.

"Do you really think that part's the climax, though?" Kevin asked. "What about when she's up in the attic?"

"Well, that's what I'm saying, kind of?"

"You know the part I mean, right? Where she's got the knife?"

"'You killed her as you tried to kill my mind,'" I recited. "'Without pity—without pity you killed her as I can kill... Kill! Kill!'"

"That part's so sweet! Anyway—" He looked down at the newsletter, freshly printed on a folded pink page. "I don't know... Like, do you actually believe this?"

I shrugged. "Not really."

Kevin laughed, popped a Jujube. "Still! It sounds legit. No, seriously! *Though the dramatic logic of the explicit story is flimsy,*" he read, "Gaslight *matters because it makes an argument for the drama of the feminine interior unusual in midcentury film.*" He put a paternal arm around me. "Didn't I say you should be a TA?"

"Whatever," I answered. Nonetheless, I did as the kid instructed. I applied to graduate school for real the next fall, and I used a version of that essay as my writing sample.

9.

I went to school, I went to sleep. But sometimes I didn't sleep. Sometimes I stayed up studying silver films on another screen, trains flickering underneath me, all around me, frame by frame. I'd moved uptown by now, and was subletting some grandmother's apartment near the UN. She'd decamped for assisted living without moving a single piece of furniture, so I slept in her teak and cane bed (a Risom original perhaps?), my laptop balanced on a pink chenille coverlet, the E train seeming to move up and through my walls, to move my fingers across the keys. *Invisible transhistorical feminist aesthetics!* I typed. *Hyperperformance as a means toward gender nihilism!* After enough such nights, my writing sample became a dissertation.

And in the years that followed, that dissertation became a book. *You Must Not Forget the Past!: New Interpretations of Old*

Heroines (Chick Crit Press, 201-). Today, the book is ranked #321,686, 422,739,127,643,998,030,772,649,222,126,037,177,832,150,889,498,772, 164,009 on Amazon. The chapter on *Gaslight* has been published separately, in a compendium of film criticism, currently ranked #9,228,756,092,662,720,815,751,821,679. The chapter in which I argue that Rosalind Russell weeps at the end of *His Girl Friday* out of frustrated pleasure at her own hard-won passivity rather than the ostensible marital bliss was cited not so many months ago in—wait for it!—*Text*. Of course I can't get a decent job. But I'm a professional, finally: a scholar and defender of the ingénue, an activator of every unresisting lass I lay my eyes on, a damsel in defense of the least deserving damsels in distress.

10.

I wish I could stop with that sequence. Finish not with a bang or a smash or a crash, but with a woman alone in a room—alone with her lying mind, no protection. But if I ended my little epic here, I wouldn't be telling the whole truth. So: forgive one final rewind?

For years the hero wanders, destiny driving her on, but all it takes is the press of a button and she's walking back-back-backward, pulling her dog back too. Rewind, and the crowd around her reverses its progress, follows in the pawsteps of its own regressive dogs. Da-ta! Dogs in cones, and dogs in cutesy knit caps. Dogs who have only just doffed their sweaters for spring. Cool-cat dogs like Orson, who dance a jaunty three-step back back back. But Stop now. Play it through. It is spring: my fourth in the one true, and I've just moved uptown. I've just discovered the half-paved path that borders the East River, and on the morning in question Orson and I are wandering toward it.

A Saturday. I'd done the things one does in the city that Saturday—walking to the bodega for coffee and a bagel, walking back to the grandmother's to brush bagel and coffee from teeth. Then? I looped a leash around Orson, and walked some more—thinking all the while, as walkers are wont to do. That Saturday, my mind was on Mary, the new girl at the movie theater. Mary from Minnesota—that was how she'd introduced herself. I still worked a shift or two on weekends, and the night before, we'd gone out after to celebrate Kevin's twenty-fifth birthday. Mary was only nineteen, but Kevin knew a place on University that didn't card. A wall-mounted television in the corner, some floodlit game falling down from on high. I stared into the green blur of a field, into a ponytailed coed's manic screaming face. I hadn't been to a bar since the Tuesday in question.

Mary from Minnesota, on the other hand, must have been to several already. Because one moment, she was sitting in the booth across from me, head lolling. The next, she was standing up, yelling over Kevin's head at no one we could see, "Yeah? Well, why don't you shut the fuck up?" Her face had filled with a wonderful, reckless light. "Asshole," she cried. "Dick."

Fifteen minutes before, Mary from Minnesota had told me she baked gingerbread with her mother every Christmas, built sweet brown houses with heart-shaped windows in the walls. Sometimes, their candy houses were four stories high! But now Mary from Minnesota was throwing her drink at some unknown nemesis beyond us, laughing bitterly as the vodka arced and split.

"Whoa! What's the story, Mary?" Kevin snuck a delighted glance at me, mouthed, "How did we get here?" We looked back at Mary—was she going to cry on us? But she was staring into some bleary distance, a wild relieved smile on her face, as if she'd just remembered something, a secret she'd kept even from herself. "Fuck you!" she said to the crowd that hedged our table, snickering. Mary didn't care. She wasn't smiling anymore, but the glitter in her gaze was glorious.

In order to reach the river, you had to cross an overpass on 63rd. The stairs were steep, difficult for Orson, and I let him rest when we got to the top. I stared down at the FDR, watched the improbable sea of surging cars, those hazy waves of red, blue, black, and silver. Orson stood still, watching with me.

Hadn't been to a bar, hadn't driven a car since the Tuesday in question. Mine was sitting in my parents' driveway still, the silver Olds I'd learned on back in 1996, swinging oblongs through the high-school parking lot with my mother or father. Only my mother would let me drive all the way home. The first time I was terrified. But she forced me to keep my foot on the gas, spin the dial toward forty-ugh, my age now.

"It's too fast!" I cried. "It doesn't feel that way when you do it. But it does when I do!"

"It *is* fast," she said. "Don't forget that."

An oil truck, a minivan, so many black sedans. I could feel their speed inside my feet, matching the red race in my veins. I could feel something else in me, too. 1996, 2006, 1986. The past crashing into the present. Don't forget, my mother said, but I had. I had forgotten.

Orson was tugging at his leash. We walked a few slanted steps, stopped. I was thinking of my mother and Mary from Minnesota, and I was thinking of my grandmother, too, her headlights sweeping those boxes she'd labeled so neatly with the years—1949, 1969—don't forget, Betty—her headlights shining a spotlight onto her own singing face. I was thinking of my grandmother—who really never should have been driving!—and I was wondering if everyone in the world agrees that the highway sounds like the sea, and maybe that's why I didn't hear him, at first.

II.

Disappointed?

12.

But after so much reinvention, could I really revise the fundamental plot? Could I kill it as you tried to kill my mind? Could I find a way to take back the language, make all the bad old words new? (Good luck with that, bitch!) I did, I still do—do it exceptionally well—do it like a professional—but what of this sad fact: the old meanings keep playing, too?

13.

Orson made his sound. *Herrrrrrrrr... Errrrrrrrr...*
    I turned. It was a bright day, but cloudy too, the sun a dull dime in the sky. I bridged my hand over my eyes.

14.

Oh how I wish I could stop! But would it even satisfy you to leave off here, staring into my stare? To leave me on the overpass, still but for the rocketing thoughts distorting my ingénue's visage? No hero for this hero, no relief? No scene partner to ask after the tear forming once more in the corner of my eye?
    Like, do you actually believe that?

15.

He was wearing ragged jeans, a thin black t-shirt with white lettering across the chest, too flaked or faded to read. He was handsome, dark, tall. He seemed about my age. His footsteps made a soft *sh sh sh...* But then he stopped. "What happened?" he asked, kindly.

16.

Disappointed?
    Think how I felt!

17.

After all, the warm wind was playing tricks on his hair. He looked right at me. "What happened?"
    I didn't know the future. I just knew that I was flushed, clammy. That I hadn't needed my sweater, after all. This man with the windy hair and bare arms was looking at me, and I didn't know yet about the several thousand days and nights we'd spend together. I might have guessed, but I didn't know how many times I'd drift from some essential action—an article I needed to write or read, an email flaring up on my radiant, terrifying screen—to ask him if he needed anything. I didn't know I'd put my fingers in his hair in an effort to play the wind's tricks, the flick of irritation I'd feel if he flicked those fingers away, the outrage that would come if he took me up on any of my many offers—yes, he did want a sandwich, and he did want me to call the plumber or his mother, and he did want me to move to Seattle Santa Cruz St. Louis with him, or just a little bit to the left because he was seriously falling off the bed. The email was from E, would I write the exhibition text for her latest dioramist? The email was from Senator J, did I want my tax dollars going straight to yet another silent weapons-shipment?—but, yes, this man did want me to look over another draft for him, this was the last time, he swore! And, yes, he did want the rest of my burger, and he did want what I wanted, of course he wanted me to be fertile and never grow old, who wouldn't? And of course he wanted me to edit the email he was writing, or pay for my share of the house, or highlight my hair, or tell him what I

wanted; shave my bikini line, share the blanket, how did I know?

How did I know who the author actor pitcher soldier senator was—had he told me? He wanted to quiz me. He wanted to hold me. He wanted to have and to hold me. He wanted to move forward, and he wanted to bring me along. Didn't I want that, too?

18.

I didn't know. Didn't know I'd wake in the dark and feel saved by the sight of his back, a blue hump in our marriage bed—*worship is the key, the absolute key*. I didn't know I'd remind myself at times like these to pretend I'd changed even if I hadn't, to pretend to be less pliable and desirous than I was; I didn't know the lengths I'd go—the futile, obvious lengths—to disguise the fact that I'd do anything for him.

But I would do anything—anything, anything, because on some level—and I don't know where I learned this, I can't just tell stories of mothers and grandmothers anymore, stories of Greek gods or Grecos—I thought I was supposed to. Or maybe that's my worst lie. Maybe I indulged my epic passivity only because it was the easiest thing.

19.

On the overpass, I didn't know my future. I didn't know that I would be a mother, too. Didn't know this man would give me a daughter, at last. Didn't know what it would feel like to smash my wineglass on that same old table once she was in bed, to watch the shards spark and settle in her toys. Her wooden truck, her My First Purse, her pitcher's mitt, her pink giraffe. I didn't know that this smashing would feel like my best correction, my first correct action, because I didn't want to do what this man was asking, or what I was offering, and hadn't we skipped a step somewhere, wasn't it my turn to rage with impunity—because, well, girls will be girls? I both knew and didn't know what it would feel like to want her hands on that glass—her tiny hands!—to want only what was best for her, to want and not want her to get every delicate cut. I didn't know what it would feel like to see the glitter on the teak, on the mess I'd picked up and piled there—her play pizza and play spatula—her little picnic basket, so many slivers stuck inside the wicker. I didn't know yet how it would feel to hear him say, "Are you fucking insane," to realize there was only one response.

I'm sorry!

That was wrong, I'm drunk, I'm sorry—

I will pick up every piece, pick up this one, pick up that one, they will never ever hurt her, she will never ever know

Because, on the overpass, his breath was warm weather on my forehead. And I answered, not knowing the man had six scars on his back—moles—he'd had moles removed, that was all—how he wished he could tell a more romantic story!

He wished, I wished. I didn't know about the wishing yet to come. I just knew that he was asking me a question.

"What happened," he said, "to your dog?"

"I did it," I said.

And he cocked his head. Looked at me as if we were partners in some ancient joke—as if we were in on some sweet and eternal conspiracy.

"You say that," he said, "like you're proud."

20.

Disappointed?
Good.
I'm glad.

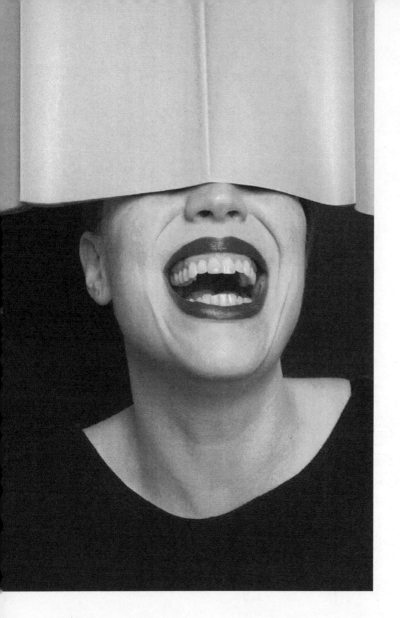

Lindsey White
She Laughs, 2018
Archival pigment print, 62.2 x 76.2 cm / 24.5 x 30 in

CREDITS

Visual Effects

© Frank Ward, Courtesy the artist

© Erio Piccagliani, Courtesy Teatro alla Scala

© Madeline McDonnell

© Cindy Sherman, Courtesy the artist and Hauser & Wirth

© PA Images

© Lindsey White, Courtesy the artist

!¡An honor to converse with these images¡!

Art direction by the steadfast and impeccable Sevy Perez

Textual Effects

Betty watches many movies or near-movies within this wannabe movie musical. Lines are quoted or adapted from *F for Fake*, *Lucia di Lammermoor*, *How to Marry a Millionaire*, *Magnificent Obsession*, *Imitation of Life*, and *The Lady from Shanghai*. Lines from *Gaslight* (1944) in particular, flicker in and out of Betty's consciousness and on and off many of these pages. Though she never mentions them explicitly, Danielle Darrieux and Vittorio De Sica are ever twirling through her mind, thanks to Max Ophüls's swirling vision in *The Earrings of Madame de...*

Betty's translation of the passage describing the death of Argos from Homer's *Odyssey* was completed with assistance from translations of the same passage by Stephen Mitchell and Emily Wilson.

Betty's *ha ha ha*s are obvs in conversation with Lorrie Moore's, as all legit *ha ha ha*s must be.

Editorial Effects

Kevin González, Edan Lepucki, Brad Liening, Kathryn Lynch, Robert McDonnell

Intrepid Interrobanging and Irreproachable Interrobang-Interrogation by Alyssa Perry

Okay, fine, Nick, you were right about everything

Stunts

Sarah Shun-lien Bynum, Tim Day, Amber Dermont, Dy, Stuart Dybek, Paul Esposito, Julia Fierro, Emily Flouton, Michele Glazer, Chris Goodmann (inimitable and excellent essence in the second *n*), Lindsay Hunter, all my Iowa young writers, Rayna Jensen, Danny Khalastchi (reading and rescuing for two decades, thank god), Miranda Kross, Edan Lepucki again (the O.L.G.), Stephen Lovely, Amy Margolis, Sabrina Orah Mark, Tim(bo) Peltason, Loretta Rodriguez, Dahlia Seroussi, Jeremy Snodgrass, Jordan Stein, Emma Uriarte, the wunderkinds in my 2016, 2019, and 2023 PSU "Rising Above Rising Action" seminars, Leni Zumas

No animals were harmed in the writing of this novel!

Best Boys

Melissa Blackall, Caren Dybek, Jody Peltason, Jessica St. John, Ruiyan Xu

Craft Services

Chez Gartho

Pyrotechnician, Stalwart

Vinnie Wilhelm

The Colosseum
The Louvre Museum
George's-Buffet Bonnet
Inger Christensen Sonnet
Nimble Tread on the Feet of Fred
Astaire to my Rogers
(I'll track you til we're codgers!)
Hilary to my Zach
Jameson to my Guinness Back
Lawfully Wedded Wife
Collaborator for Life
Michael Jordan to my Bobby Hansen
CP to my MM

Caryl Pagel (thank you forever)

Executive Producers

Mome, Dade, Michael (aka Christoph D.), Leo (aka *Brah*-ther!),
Grandmas MLL & AVM, Grandpas FWL & HEM

Veronica, Charlie, Nick